Justice at Blackwater

JUSTICE AT BLACKWATER

Terrell L. Bowers

AVALON BOOKS
THOMAS BOUREGY AND COMPANY, INC.
401 LAFAYETTE STREET
NEW YORK, NEW YORK 10003

© Copyright 1990 by Terrell L. Bowers
Library of Congress Catalog Card Number: 89-81640
ISBN 0-8034-8794-0

PRINTED IN THE UNITED STATES OF AMERICA
BY HADDON CRAFTSMEN, SCRANTON, PENNSYLVANIA

Justice at Blackwater

Prologue

*T*he ship was tossed about on the violent waves. Rain and wind gusted through the cracks of the cabin. Men shouted back and forth as the whitecaps splashed over the bow.

Orem Clancy, not yet eight years old, huddled in a corner with his mother. The terrible thundering against the cabin, the pounding of water against the hull—the noise was deafening.

"Dearborne!" his mother cried. "What's happening? Are we going to sink?"

Orem's father was at the window. There was no glass, only wooden shutters. He kept watch, prepared to abandon ship and attempt to save his family—should the need arise.

"More trouble," he said grimly. "Yonder comes a Navy ship. We have slaves on board."

"The authorities won't think we are involved with anything like that, will they?"

"I've got my papers to show why we took this vessel. We'll be all right."

"Unless the ship capsizes!" She was more frightened than Orem had ever seen her.

"We won't be able to outrun or outmaneuver that Navy ship. The ocean is too rough. We have to keep the bow into the waves or we'll capsize."

"How far to land?"

"Can't see any lights or shoreline yet. I'd say we're still several miles out to sea."

Men hollered on deck. There was the sound of running feet and the scramble of people moving about. Orem sat up straight, listening to the sounds in the night.

"Looks like something's going on." Dearborne was peering out against the pelting rain and blowing wind.

Although only a boy, Orem always gave in to a curious nature. It was hard to stay put and not see what was happening. He left the comfort of his mother's arms to stand alongside his father. By putting his eye to a narrow crack, he could see the deck.

Using whips and clubs, several men were driving a bunch of men, women, and children out into the rain. Orem knew that if he repeated the words they used, he would get his mouth washed out with soap.

"Good Heavens!" Orem's father said. "They aren't going to. . . ."

Orem stared at the scene, aghast. He had seen a lot of black people before. There were a number of plantations near his home. However, these were different from those slaves. They wore only animal-skin loincloths and spoke an odd-sounding language he did not understand. By pressing hard, he could see their faces—children crying, women cradling their babies, men with fearful, wide eyes.

All of the adults wore shackles, and a single chain bound them all together. They were herded along the deck to the railing. Several men lashed them with whips, driving them along the bucking deck. They were a frightened group, holding on to one another, wet and cold from the driving rain.

When they reached the rail, two big men pushed the first three or four over the side of the ship. The weight from those few jerked the others to the rail, and they were dragged over as well. The wails, the terrified shrieks rang in Orem's ears.

"God forgive my weakness," Dearborne said reverently, his voice cracking. "There is nothing I can do."

Orem felt his own eyes burn with tears. One little girl broke and ran toward their cabin. She was grabbed roughly and tossed into the murky darkness of the water, screaming. The wind and the slap of the ocean waves silenced her cries.

Orem could not look away. Some of the slaves clung to the railing or one another, trying desperately to survive. He watched the brutal crew move along the string of people with clubs. They beat them until they could no longer hang on. Soon the last of them had been swallowed up by the darkness and the sea.

"What are they doing, Dearborne?" his mother asked. "What's going on?"

Orem's father hung his head. "They sent all those African people to watery graves. The Navy won't be able to prove that there were any slaves on board."

"We can tell," Orem said. "We saw it, Papa. We can tell them what happened."

"It would mean our lives, son. These slavers would kill us if we came forward with the truth."

"But . . . but all of those people. They can't swim in the water. They will drown!"

Dearborne placed his hand on Orem's shoulder. He looked very old and tired. There was an incredible sadness in his face.

"It's over and done. We can't help them now."

Orem felt sick inside. "You mean they're all gonna die—even that little girl?"

"The storm has about blown itself out." Dearborne did not answer his question. "The whitecaps are almost gone."

"What about the Navy ship?" Orem's mother wanted to know.

"They are coming alongside."

"Do we forget what we saw?"

"We have no choice. Try to put it out of your minds."

"I can't forget," Orem said, filled with an emptiness he could not comprehend. "I'll never forget."

Chapter One

*I*t was not far to the river. If he could
make it across to Texas, he would have a
chance to escape. There would be a horse
he could steal, a wagon in which he could
hide. He would somehow find a way to get
into Mexico.

But Togg Jackson had run full out for
twenty miles. He was staggering, too
winded to continue. His lungs were on fire,
his legs too weak to hold up his weight any
longer. He spilled onto the grass and lay
there, gasping for breath. The sun beat
down unmercifully on his bare, bronze
torso, the sweat trickling down his brow
and from his shoulders and back. He was
exhausted from the long, desperate run.

Togg rolled his head from side to side.
He had come so far. He had to find the

strength to get back up. If Master Colensworth caught him, he would be beaten to death. No slave had ever escaped Master Baldwin Colensworth, not ever.

With a sudden fear encrusting his heart like a glove of ice, he rose to a sitting position. He turned his head and put an ear into the slight breeze. Was that the sound of a distant horse? Was it the baying of dogs?

Shielding his eyes from the glare of the midday sun, Togg tried to see back over his trail. The sweltering heat waves distorted his vision, making everything look unreal. It was full summer in Louisiana, hot and humid. Even the snakes and lizards were seeking shelter from the sun this time of year.

A dust devil danced across the open expanse, swirling its circular pattern as if to a wild song. It faded quickly, for the air was heavy, the burning heat too intense even for a whirlwind to survive.

Togg was up again, his legs unsteady, his shoulders bowed against the sun's relentless rays. His mouth felt as if it was full of dust, his eyes grating in their sockets. He trudged onward, aimless in his direction, uncertain of where the river was. He knew only that he had to get away.

His mind laughed at his efforts, while his body cried out for relief. How stupid he was. It was ludicrous to defend his life so devoutly. After all, what had Togg ever known in his life but misery? Why was he so desperate to live?

From the day the raiders had come into his African village, Togg had known only suffering and sorrow. Even after ten years, he could recall the stench of the cargo hold and the agony of watching men die in their chains. His own father had grown sick on the way to America and died shortly after they had landed. He had been brought over with his parents and brother and little sister, but his sister had been sold to a different buyer. There had been endless weeks on that stinking death ship, suffering the filth that mingled with sweaty and diseased bodies. The water had been tepid, the food rotten and inedible. No wonder his father had succumbed to death. Togg survived to watch his mother forced to take a husband she did not want; she died trying to give birth at forty years of age. He had watched the other young men sold off to different plantations to toil in the fields and father another generation of field slaves. Lastly, and not so long ago, he had watched his own brother beaten to death for daring to look at Master Baldwin Colensworth's wife, Roweena.

That was the most bitter memory. The white woman played a horrible game with the slaves. If ever there was a woman who loved to watch other men suffer, it was the wife of The Bull of Louisiana.

She had a black servant girl who was the holder of Togg's heart. Roweena had her suspicions about the two of them, but she had never caught them exchanging longing glances or speaking softly when no one could hear. If the woman knew of their special fondness, she would have used it against both of them. They would have become a new game for her.

As for Baldwin, he was of the old way. He believed that a slave should never lift his eyes to look him in the face, but should bow before him like a cowed dog. When he had caught Togg's brother watching his wife, he had ordered the beating that had meant his death. Naturally, Roweena had been there to watch.

Now the ground seemed to go out from under Togg. Only his quick hands prevented the earth from coming up to slap him in the face. Togg found himself lying on his stomach, gasping hard to draw in air. He was totally spent. If he did not find sanctuary, he would die.

Even as he tried to regain enough energy to continue his flight, the terrible sound of pounding hooves reached his ears. Togg rose up, but he was unable to get away. Three men surrounded him at once. He was caught!

Orem Clancy pulled Tumbleweed to a stop and watched for a moment. He could see three men using their ropes, swinging the ends brutally downward at something. At first he thought it was a game, that they were hazing a steer or wild animal. When he saw the black man try to run, a knot twisted within his gut.

He put his heels to his skittish animal and was rewarded with two jumps to the side before Tumbleweed responded and went the right direction.

The man on foot wore no shirt. His back and shoulders were streaked with blood. The three riders had been using the ropes like whips, beating the poor man until he could hardly see where he was going.

Orem's horse bolted into the group and inadvertently knocked the slave to the ground. The three men broke off their assault and lined up opposite Orem. Two wore cowboy hats and clothes, while the biggest of the three wore overalls and looked like a man who spent most of his time ripping out trees by their roots. Orem had one advantage by having his hands free. All of them still held the ends of their ropes and the reins of their horses.

"Appears to me that the dark fellow here has had enough, boys." Orem offered a peaceful smile. Three-to-one odds did not promote overconfidence. "I'm not one to interfere with anyone else's business, but I'm a little curious as to what the man did. He kill someone?"

"Keep your nose out of this, stranger," one man warned.

"Ain't none of your affair, nohow," another said.

But Orem had never learned to stay away from trouble. The black man was on his knees, haggard and barely conscious, his mouth open to draw in air. Another five minutes of being beaten with ropes and he would be dead.

Orem slowly looked the three men over. They were all wearing guns, but not one had the thong off the hammer. If it came to a gunfight, he could take all three before they got one pistol free of the holster. It was something they also seemed to realize.

Orem rested his hand over his .36 Spiller and Burr revolver. Reflecting a calm he did not feel, he smiled a second time at the group.

"No need for there to be any hard feelings over this, fellows. If this here gent murdered someone in his sleep, I'll be glad to help you string him up."

The three exchanged looks, then one of them took charge. He puffed out his chest. "I'm Clay Douglas, stranger. This here is Matt Lamount and Lars Sweeny. We all hail from the Diamond Head Plantation. You ever hear of that?"

Orem emitted a long whistle. "The Diamond Head—Baldwin Colensworth's cotton plantation."

"That's right," Clay said with a smirk. "Now you don't want old man Colensworth on your back, do you?"

"He's a powerful man up here in Louisiana," Orem acknowledged.

"You bet," the one called Matt Lamount said. "If you want your gizzard roasted over an open fire, you mess with The Bull of Louisiana."

"He send you to kill this man?"

"Runaway slave." Clay showed open contempt. He paused to spit at the slave's feet. "Got to teach his kind a lesson."

"Well, I'm a peace-loving man, boys. I don't want any trouble."

"Then you'd best move on," Lars told him. "We'll handle things for Mr. Colensworth."

To ride away might be signing the young black man's death warrant. Orem did some quick thinking.

"You know, I'd sure like to meet The

Bull personally. Would you mind if I rode back with the four of you?"

The men exchanged looks, then Clay shrugged. "I think that'd be a good idea, stranger. We've given Togg a taste of discipline. I imagine Mr. Colensworth will want to dish out the weasel's punishment himself."

Orem felt as if he had backed into a cactus patch blindfolded. If he got careless, he might wind up with a tail full of thorns. He wasn't popular around the neighboring plantations. Too many of the owners knew about him.

Little late to worry, he thought to himself. *I'm committed now. A man's life is at stake.*

The man named Togg was thrown over the back of Matt's horse. Then all five of them rode toward Diamond Head. Orem naturally fell in at the rear of the group. He did not want any of the three men from the Diamond Head at his back.

A vision from the past haunted his memory. As he caught Togg's perplexed glance, he remembered a stormy night on the sea.

He could again visualize the fearful eyes, the faces that were masks of terror. Try as he might, he could not ignore Togg's misery.

Chapter Two

*B*aldwin Colensworth was an older man, with silver hair, dark eyes, and too many pounds at his middle. He had been a large man in his youth, but the years had bowed his shoulders and allowed his powerful chest to slip. He met the riders at the porch of a huge house. He paused to lean against one of the massive columns and narrowly regarded the runaway slave, his three men, and lastly Orem Clancy.

The slave was shoved off the horse at the edge of the porch. He rose up to his hands and knees, but lacked the strength to stand. His head was low enough that his hair touched the soft dust at the foot of the steps.

"You were warned, Togg," Baldwin told

17

the black man. "You're cut from the same cloth as your brother, rotten to your soul."

"Don't kill me, Master Colensworth," the slave pleaded softly without raising his head.

Baldwin again put his burning eyes on Orem. "What is your business here, young fella?"

Orem knew that the wrong words might get him killed. The odds against him had not improved, for the men were on two sides and ready for trouble. A man who used his wits before resorting to violence, Orem decided to try diplomacy. If it came to a gunfight, he was going to have to kill or be killed.

"I'm looking for a groom for my father's stables. I thought you might be willing to part with this worthless specimen for a reasonable price."

"He butted in while we were teaching Togg a lesson about running away," Clay informed Baldwin. "I think he's one of them John Brown types."

Baldwin smiled, but it was a sarcastic smirk. "John Brown was hanged, young fella. That should be an important lesson to men who think like that maniac. We don't look kindly on people telling us what we can do with our stock."

It grated against Orem's nerves that the man referred to his slaves as stock. However, he hid his displeasure, putting a congenial smile on his face.

"A smart businessman would always rather make a few dollars than bury a profit. I would think that you might want to sell this man rather than kill him. If he's a troublemaker, I've got men who can control him—without beating him to death. Handling some of these people is like taming a wild stallion. It ain't how much you beat them, it's how you break them."

Baldwin's face grew dark. "Who are you to compare a field slave to a fine horse?" He frowned and took a step forward. "I think Clay is right. I believe you are a Northern sympathizer, boy. And let me tell you, someone who advocates the Abe Lincoln sort of thinking in Louisiana is looking to end up dangling from a noose."

The three men tensed as one, all ready to pull their guns and start shooting. Orem was none too pleased to be the only target available, so he offered his inoffensive smile.

"I hail from Kanterville, Mr. Colensworth. I imagine you've heard of the Honeysuckle Plantation?"

That opened his eyes. "You come from there?"

"I've a ranch thereabouts. Suffice to say, Frank Ambrose and I are good friends."

Baldwin's face underwent an immediate transformation. He was suddenly all smiles.

"Well, that's different, son. Why don't y'all come in for something cool to drink? It's mighty hot out in the sun."

Orem knew when to raise a hand and when to fold. This was a time to call the bet and sit tight. He had a little money on him. There might be a way to save the slave from a beating that could possibly kill him.

"What about Togg here?" Matt wanted to know.

Baldwin grunted in open contempt. "The tanning shed is a good spot. Put him there for a while. I imagine he needs a little rest."

Orem dismounted and tied up his horse.

Then he followed Baldwin into the house. He was careful to remove his hat.

"George," Baldwin said to an elderly, white-haired slave, "tell Sarah to bring us each a mint julep. We'll be in the drawing room."

"Yes, sir," George replied softly.

Baldwin's house was one of the most luxurious Orem had ever seen. A spiral staircase, a thick rug in the middle of the polished hardwood floors, fine draperies, paintings on the wall, a great fireplace in the drawing room, and imported furniture from around the world all proved that the plantation owner was a wealthy man.

Baldwin led the way into the drawing room. "Have a seat, Mr. . . ." He paused. "What did you say your name was?"

"Orem Clancy. My father is Dearborne Clancy."

Recognition showed in the man's eyes. "Ah, yes, owner of several banks, including the one at Blackwater."

"That's right."

Baldwin sat down in a rosewood chair, so Orem rested his haunches on a sofa with a scroll-curved back. The conversation died until a young, attractive black woman entered with two drinks. She set one on the table next to Baldwin and handed the other to Orem.

"Thank you, ma'am," he said out of habit. She blinked in surprise and left the room quickly.

"You needn't say thank you to servants, Mr. Clancy. They have a tendency to forget their place as it is."

"No harm meant," he responded quickly. "I spend a lot of time visiting customers. It's a practice to be polite."

Colensworth looked hard at Orem. Despite Colensworth's advanced years, Orem realized that this man could be a tiger. He was not deceived by Orem's ruse about buying a slave, not one bit.

"I could have let my men kill you, Mr. Clancy. Clay and Matt are good shots. As for Lars, it would take two or three shots to kill a man as big as him."

Orem took a sip of the drink and smiled. "The thought occurred to me. That Lars would make a fair-sized bull."

"So why do you want to meddle in my affairs?"

"I don't intend any trouble, Mr. Colensworth. I'm a peace-loving man. My offer to buy the slave is a genuine one. I would rather purchase him than have him killed senselessly."

"What an odd set of values you have. I find that it is necessary from time to time to demonstrate to these black children that we are their keepers. When they try to escape, they are punished. It is the only treatment they understand."

"Slaves are human beings too, Mr. Colensworth. It makes no sense to kill them when you can still turn a profit. I'm offering to buy that young man from you."

"The answer is no. I have to make an impression on the others. If an example costs me a two-thousand-dollar investment, I think it is worth the expense." The man's voice was calm and controlled. As he finished, he met Orem with a hard stare. "Besides, Mr. Clancy, I have heard of you. I believe you have been stirring up the slavery issue for some years." Orem did not deny his accusation, so he continued. "You have managed to set free a few slaves, adding to the unrest of those still in their proper station. If we don't watch out for these children, they will be lost. You are tampering with the balance of nature, Clancy. It is men like you who put Lincoln in office. You will be responsible for the downfall of our country."

Orem knew when he was up against a stone wall. He let out a sigh and took another drink. Then he rose to his feet.

"I'll take no more of your time, Mr. Colensworth. I've a long ride ahead of me."

The man did not bother to rise himself. "Good day to you, sir. I hope one day you come to your senses. Slaves are not people. They are stock. They must be nurtured and tended. If you persist in freeing them to run about, they will turn on us like rabid dogs."

Orem wordlessly left the house. Clay was standing on the porch. He grinned at Orem and cocked his head toward a nearby building.

"Your dark friend is going to soak up the sun till he rots. If you ever come onto Diamond Head again, you'll be right at his side." He stood tall, eyes like chinks of ice. "Understand?"

Orem didn't like being threatened, but he did not know where Clay's two friends were lurking. Better to swallow a little pride than be buried under six feet of earth.

"I hear you."

"Ride out, slave-lover. Ride out and don't look back."

Orem did as the man instructed. He glanced at the tanning shed and saw Togg strapped to the wall, exposed to the burning sun. As he was already dried out from his escape attempt, he would wilt like a stalk of corn without water. No one would dare offer him anything to eat or drink. He would die there, murdered for his desire to be a free man. There was nothing anyone could do to save him, nothing at all.

Orem nudged Tumbleweed with his heels. The horse sidestepped, jumped forward, then opened up into an easy lope. In a matter of seconds, Orem was passing the open fields of cotton. It would be dark in a couple of hours. That was when he would make a move. He had an idea what his father would say about his going up against a powerful man like Baldwin Colensworth, but he had to do what he thought was right—regardless of what it cost.

Chapter Three

*T*ogg could not swallow. His lips were dry and cracked, his tongue swollen so much it felt like cotton. With his arms stretched out, holding him up off the ground, his muscles cried out for relief. His wrists ached from the ropes, while his hands were numb. The sun had finally gone down, so he had some relief from the burning rays, but he was dying. As sure as he was bound to the side of the shed, he would die there.

Even as he contemplated what death would have to offer a slave, he opened his eyes to mere slits. He saw Sarah come out the back of the house. She was scraping leftovers to the dogs.

His mouth began to contract, searching for enough moisture to water his taste buds. His stomach growled and twisted into a knot. He could smell the fried chicken from the night's meal. It was sheer torture to see the dogs gobbling up scraps for which he would have gladly traded an arm or leg.

Twisting his head slightly, he clenched his teeth. When he heard soft steps, he glanced around to see Sarah a few feet away.

She hesitated, quickly looking around, then whispered, "If I can, I'll bring you something—once everyone is asleep."

He slowly shook his head from side to side. She would only get herself in trouble. Togg was a man, he could die like a man. There was no need for Sarah to get involved. Her frail body could never withstand the whip.

"D-don't." He managed the single word in a hoarse whisper.

"Why'd you do it, Togg?" She was near tears. "Why'd you run away?"

He worked to swallow and ran his thick tongue over his chapped lips. Even so, it was impossible to speak clearly.

"Gotta be . . . free," he said. "M-Mexico. . . ."

"It's over five hundred miles to Mexico! You dumb donkey! How'd you expect to get that far?"

He shook his head again. "You're beautiful, Sarah."

She stamped her foot in the dirt. "You dumb donkey! You're dumb, dumb, dumb!"

Togg didn't have to tell her that he would have come back for her. It was all a romantic, impossible dream. But he knew that he would have learned to be a free man in Mexico, his own man. He would have practiced with a gun and hired himself an army to ride at his side. With rumors of a possible war between the Southern and the Northern states over the slavery issue, he could have found allies. He would have come back and taken the girl he loved. He and Sarah would have started a life together, a life as free people.

Suddenly, a man came out of the dark. It was Matt Lamount. Before Sarah could escape, he grabbed her by the arms.

"Well, look what we got here." He

laughed, turning his attention toward Togg. "Is this what they call a clandestine romance?"

Togg did not know what that big word meant, but if it came from Matt's lips, it was dirt. He strained at the ropes that held him, using what little strength he had left.

"Let go of me!" Sarah was bold against the field boss.

Matt did as he pleased with the pickers and workers of the fields, but he did not often cross the line. The house servants were not his to command. In fact, George, the old head servant, had told him more than once to get out of the house.

"You're mighty uppity for a slave." Matt laughed at her struggles. "I've a mind to teach you a lesson."

"Don't you touch her!" Togg's voice had no strength. He pulled at the ropes, but it was a waste of effort.

Matt laughed again. It was then Togg realized that the man was drunk. That accounted for his nerve. Sober, he never would have tried anything against any of the house servants. Colensworth expected those people to be treated decently.

"Always hiding behind those big walls and fancy curtains, ain't you, Sarah? Always safe from the burning sun and blistering heat. Serve your mistress and be spared real work."

"Master Baldwin will have you tacked up on the shed next to Togg if you don't let go of me! You'd better think about that, white trash!" Sarah cried. She might have bluffed her way through, but not by calling Matt a name. He didn't take that from any slave—house servant or field hand.

Togg was helpless to act. Matt spun Sarah around and slapped her hard. She staggered backward and fell to the ground. Before she could scream, the man grabbed her, holding her arms at her sides.

"Now, Miss High-and-Mighty, you can beg my forgiveness. If I believe you, I might let you go and not tell your master that you were out here trying to sneak food and water to Togg. You wouldn't be so pretty after a whipping." He snickered. "How about we start by you giving me a big kiss?"

"How about you give this a big kiss?"

a voice said, and a shadowy figure came out of the dark.

When Matt looked up, the flat stock of a rifle smacked him right in the face. It knocked him over onto his back, and he was out cold.

Orem didn't have time for small talk. He drew his skinning knife and cut the ropes that held Togg.

"Come on, fella. We've got to get out of here."

Togg could hardly stand up, but he took a moment to lend a hand up to the girl. For a split second, they were in each other's arms. Then Orem took hold of him and led the way to his horse and the mare he had borrowed from Colensworth's stables. There would not be much time before the alarm was sounded. In the dark, they needed only a few minutes' head start. That would be enough to escape Baldwin Colensworth's plantation.

After pausing long enough for Togg to gulp a few swallows of water, the two of them rode silently through the darkness. It was a mile past the river before the slave rode up alongside Orem.

"Why did you risk your life for me?" he wanted to know. "You're a white man."

"The color of a man's skin shouldn't dictate whether he's a good man, a bad man, a master, or a slave, Togg. For every white like Colensworth there are a thousand like me who believe in justice and the equality of man," Orem responded.

Even in the dark, he could see Togg's incredulous expression. The man had known only slavery most of his life. Raised among the cruel taskmasters on Diamond Head, he naturally assumed that all white people were alike.

"You saved me at the river. Matt and the others were going to beat me to death."

"I'm not in favor of killing people, especially when their only crime is wanting to be free."

"Clouting Matt with your rifle will get you thrown in jail or killed. Why risk that for me?"

Orem smiled in his direction. "Aren't you worth fighting for, Togg?"

"Not against Baldwin Colensworth. He's a powerful man. We hear talk that he

is about as powerful as the government itself."

"He might not be as big as he thinks he
is," Orem said with a shrug of indifference.
"If President Lincoln decrees that all
slaves are free, Baldwin will find himself
broke and all alone."

"I thank you, mister, for helping out
Sarah. She had her hands full with Matt.
I owe you my life three times over. You
saved me at the river, you saved me from
the tanning shed, and you saved Sarah
from Matt. How do I repay you for all
those lives?"

"We'll think of something," Orem replied easily. "First thing, we get you into
Texas. No one will come looking for you
at my ranch."

"Whatever you say, mister."

"The name is Orem Clancy. You can
call me Orem."

That arched Togg's brows. "Me? I call
you Orem?"

"I'm not a master, Togg. You can work
for me, if you've a mind to, but not as a
slave. I hire men—I don't buy them into
obedience."

"I'll do whatever you say . . . Orem."

That put a trace of a smile on Orem's lips. He doubted that Togg had ever addressed a white man by his first name. It would take Togg some getting used to, acting and talking like a free man.

But Orem had some misgivings about that. How could he deal with a man like Baldwin Colensworth? The Bull of Louisiana was not going to be easy to pacify. If Colensworth sent the U.S. Marshal after him, Orem could possibly end up in prison. There had to be a way to keep the law out of it. He would figure out a way to make things right with Colensworth. Once he was rid of that problem, he could worry about educating Togg enough that the man could become independent.

If Orem's father heard about this latest escapade, he would be coming around to see him again. Dearborne Clancy couldn't understand his son's impatience. He maintained that slavery would end with a proclamation from the President of the United States. All a person had to do was sit back and wait.

But Orem couldn't do that. He was

driven by an unseen power, compelled to help men like Togg be free. It seemed a hopeless undertaking. After all, he was only one man. Could one man make such a difference? There would always be another Baldwin Colensworth, someone who wanted to rule other people like a king. What he couldn't buy, he terrorized through his crew of bullies. To oppose a man like him could cost Orem his life. He should have forgotten all about Togg. Lincoln would soon free the slaves. It was not his battle to venture forth alone and take on The Bull of Louisiana.

That thought was cast out of his head at once. A delay of even one day would have meant death for Togg. Orem could never stand by and watch another black person die. The haunting memory was with him always. He had seen their horror-stricken faces too often at night in his dreams. He heard their cries. Time and again, he found himself reaching out, trying to take hold of that little girl's hand. She had run toward their cabin, terrified, crying. How many sleepless nights he had wished he could reach out and take her into his arms! He would have saved her.

But Dearborne had not acted. He had been afraid for the lives of his son and wife. He was a man of good conscience and moral values, but he was not a man of action. He had frozen, fearful for his family. Orem knew his father had also felt the wetness of tears and the ache in his heart. He suffered in mental anguish, but he advocated nonintervention. He maintained that the law of the land would change.

Not soon enough to suit me. Some people like Togg can't wait, he thought. What more could a man ask than that? If his conscience was clear, if he felt good in his own heart, what else mattered?

"How far are we going?" Togg broke into his contemplation.

"My ranch is about seventy miles into Texas. You stick with me and you'll have to earn your keep. Like I said before, I hire men, I don't buy them."

"You mean I'll be working for wages, like an ordinary man?"

"Once you pay off this debt. I've got to

see how much Colensworth will take to release you."

"That's easy to figure," Togg replied. "He'll want both of our lives. You crossed The Bull himself. That there man is too proud to let you or me get away. I got to thank you for saving me, but it's going to be your end."

"We'll see what happens, Togg. If Colensworth won't listen to reason, I'll find some other way to get your release."

"I don't understand you, Orem. Why all this concern for me—a slave?"

"I don't think of men as masters or slaves, Togg. I prefer to see all people as mankind."

"You've got some funny notions, Orem. I think you're going to get yourself killed off real quick."

"One day soon, you and all the other slaves will be freed, and you'll have to learn to live like free people."

"How can I learn something like that?" he asked. "I don't know anything about being a free man."

"It starts with respect for yourself and others, and with accepting the responsibility of being free. That means obeying the laws and sticking up for the rights of others."

"Yes, sir, Orem, I think I know what you're saying. But I don't feel that yet."

"It'll come with time. Once you are away from Colensworth and his kind for a spell, you'll understand."

"You're a good man, Orem. I'd be proud to work for you and learn."

There was a lightness in Orem's chest. He couldn't put a name to it, but he felt good.

Chapter Four

*J*udge Devires looked at Orem and cocked his head toward the side of the building. Orem knew the gallows were standing there, ominous, foreboding.

"You looking to get your neck stretched, Orem?" the judge asked meaningfully. "There is a law against stealing slaves or helping them to escape their lawful owners."

"I know that, Judge."

"Yet you go right ahead and do something dumb. Your father asked me to stick by you on this, but the law is the law—whether you like it or not."

"I know that, Judge. But the man would not have lived the night. Punishment of a slave has to have limitations. Show me

41

where the law condones killing a person for running away."

"Don't go nitpicking with me, Orem. The law isn't on trial here. You are the one who is risking going to prison."

Orem was alone with the judge. It was an informal meeting, only the two of them. Judge Devires was a close friend of Orem's father. He was the one man who could help Orem stay clear of a Wanted poster.

"I saw three men beating the slave with ropes. When I confronted Colensworth and asked to buy the man, he said no. Togg was to be tortured and killed as a deterrent to the other slaves. To my way of thinking, there is no law against saving a man's life."

The judge let out a long sigh. "Baldwin Colensworth has admitted that the young man was being disciplined. To his knowledge, there was no risk of permanent injury to Togg."

"There is a term for that kind of statement, Judge. It's called a bald-faced lie. Togg wouldn't have lasted the night."

"So you claim."

"That's right."

"We have to settle this some way, Orem.

Colensworth is talking about putting a price on your head. He'll do it too."

"Any man who tries to collect had better put on his climbing shoes, because I'm going to be one tall hill."

"Now, don't be talking like that. I don't want you starting a war. Bad enough that you crossed into Louisiana to start trouble."

"My bank is at Blackwater, Judge. Because of the location of the Sabine River, it happens to be in Louisiana."

"Why can't you talk to your father? Maybe he'll let you manage the banks in Texas and put another man in charge of Blackwater."

"I happen to own a share of the bank in Blackwater, Judge."

"So what am I supposed to do, Orem? Colensworth wants justice. He has demanded that I issue a warrant for your arrest."

"He has no proof that I took his slave. Is a man guilty before he has a trial?"

"Where is this slave now?"

"At my ranch."

The judge grunted. "And I'm not supposed to think you are guilty? You don't even lie to me about his whereabouts."

"I tell you, Judge, the man showed up on my doorstep. He was looking for work. I gave him a job and set out to straighten this out first off."

"And I'm to convince Colensworth of that?" He laughed without mirth. "I wonder which of us is more crazy."

"I'll still pay the man a fair price for Togg. Can't you rule on that?"

"No. The slave is not up for sale. I have only your word that his life was in imminent danger."

"The only way to prove his life was being threatened was to wait until he was dead. Then I could steal the body and you would have had to believe me."

The judge frowned, but Orem knew he believed his every word. Colensworth's name had been mentioned in a number of incidents concerning brutality to slaves. His nickname, The Bull of Louisiana, did not derive from his gentle, kindhearted nature.

"Things might be changing sooner than we both think, Orem. Have you been reading the news lately? Looks to be a real division of states over the slavery issue. With Lincoln elected as President this year, South Carolina has seceded from the Union. From what I've been able to ascertain, there are several more Southern states intent on doing the same thing in the next few months. You know what that means?"

"What's that saying? A house divided against itself can't stand?"

Judge Devires showed a worried mien. "It means war, Orem. We'll actually have a war between Americans."

"I don't know all the politics about it, Judge, but I can't take a stand against Lincoln. I've been on a lot of plantations for business reasons. Some of those slaves have an acceptable life, but I've also seen cases where some of those people are treated worse than stray dogs. I'd like to think that there is an alternative to fighting a war, but I'm for figuring we passed the point where words will do the trick."

"What are you going to do should the Southern states break off and go to war against the North?"

"Reckon every man will have to follow

his own conscience. If an invading army comes into Texas or Louisiana, like as not I'll take a gun and defend the state. If someone asked me to pack up and go to battle clear across the country, I'd probably say no thanks. I'm not the kind of man that could kill my own countrymen."

The judge smiled at him. "Funny stance to take, Orem, after some of the things I've heard about you. However, I can't argue your logic. I wouldn't want to kill my neighbors and fellow countrymen, either."

"So where does that leave you, Judge? Would you pick up arms and go to war?"

"There is a certain honor in my family. I'm a bit too old to enter the field of battle, but my son is near twenty. I'm sure he would be expected to fight for the South."

"There ain't no two ways about it—a fight between the North and the South would be a disaster. It would be brother against brother, neighbor against neighbor."

Judge Devires raised his eyebrows. "Speaking of that sort of conflict, we have a rebel in our midst who's been stirring up a lot of noise."

"That right?"

"If I get the chance, I'll introduce you. First off, we have to settle this business between you and Colensworth. You can't take him on in a fight. He's got money, power, and a worthless son who would love to shoot you in the back."

"I'm open to suggestions. Have you got any?"

"You say the alleged runaway slave is at your ranch?"

"That's right. I've two other black men who break horses working for me."

"And your place is on the Texas side?"

"Of course. Louisiana law can't touch them over there, and I've got influence in my home state."

"Thanks to your father. It does help to be the son of a man who owns three banks and knows the governor well enough to call him by his first name."

Orem grinned. "I suppose you've got a point, Judge. However, I am a man of honor. I'd still like to try to settle with Colensworth for the slave. He wouldn't sell him before, but now that he hasn't any choice, he might listen to reason."

"I wouldn't count on it."

Orem grinned. "It's the honorable thing to do."

"How about those two other men, the ones who break horses for you? How did you acquire them?"

"I didn't steal them, Judge. I purchased them."

"You bought slaves of your own?"

"Not me. I have them working off debts. Once they repay whatever I spent to purchase their contracts, they are free to go and do as they please. I sign them over to be free men."

"So they bust broncos to pay for their freedom. That's an interesting way of freeing slaves, Orem."

He grinned at the judge. "They earn every penny and learn a trade in the process."

"They any good at breaking horses?"

"Not very. They try hard, but they were field slaves. They've never been around wild animals. I picked up those horses down below the Pecos, and they're bullheaded mustang stock. Even an experienced horse wrangler would have his hands full with them."

"That one of your well-broke horses I saw you ride into town on, the one that shied away from every horse, wagon, and watering trough?"

"Tumbleweed," Orem replied. "He's coming along."

"It's a wonder he hasn't dumped you on your head in the middle of a cactus patch." The judge grunted. "Maybe he *has* dropped you on your noggin a few times too many. Why else would any man cross Baldwin Colensworth?"

"I hear his son, Jace, is a wild sort. I never met him, but I've heard some stories about him."

"He's nothing but trouble, Orem. You stay away from that one. I've heard that he killed a free black man because of the color of his skin. There was no motive other than that."

"Most blacks know better than to fight against a white man. Even a free black. Since Jace killed him, nothing was done. If the black had beaten or killed Jace, he would have been hanged on the spot."

"I guess it's the way things are at the moment. Fighting is breaking out over the issue of slavery, and there's going to be a lot more killing. That's why you've got to be careful, Orem. You can't go around rescuing every slave you come across."

"That's for sure. My ranch isn't big enough to accommodate many more workers. I'm going in the hole now. If it wasn't for my father's having me run the bank at Blackwater, I'd be broke."

"At least you had the good sense not to show up with that slave at your side. I'd have had a hard time overlooking that."

Orem grinned again. "Judge, you won't make a very good man for the South. Feeling like you do, I think you ought to move farther north."

Even as the two of them stood there, a knock came at the door. The judge glanced out and smiled at Orem.

"It's the rebel I was telling you about." He chuckled and opened the door.

A young woman entered the room. She had a pencil and a pad of paper in her hand. She offered Judge Devires a bright smile.

"Here's trouble for you, Orem," the judge said.

Orem took note of the girl's trim build, the flattering way she wore her light brown hair loose about her shoulders, and her sparkling gray-blue eyes. She boldly confronted them both.

"I presume this is the man you told me about, Judge?" She eyed Orem with a skeptical appraisal. "Funny, but you don't look much like another John Brown. There isn't any wild look about you, no beard, no long, flying hair, no piercing eyes."

"Sorry to disappoint you, ma'am," Orem said, offering her his most winning smile. "Although I don't know what I'm supposed to have in common with John Brown."

"I ran your story in my newspaper." She returned his smile. "It got me two rocks through my front window and a warning letter that was left anonymously."

Orem frowned and looked at Devires for some kind of explanation.

"Miss Jamie Kleg, meet Orem Clancy," the judge said instead.

She extended her hand, and he took it

in a short greeting. Then he looked at her curiously.

"Did you say your newspaper?"

"That's right. I put out the *Shreveport Free Press* once a week. It isn't very big yet, but I've made a few ripples."

"Not very popular ripples," Devires said with some frankness. "Jamie has a nasty habit of finding fault with the Southern states over the slavery issue. If she wasn't a woman, she'd have been killed by this time."

"I've had some threats that included warnings about printing anything against slavery," she admitted offhandedly. "It helps sell more newspapers. Hardly a person in town can wait for me to bring up the issue in my weekly column. It gives them someone to hate and talk about for the rest of the week."

"I keep telling her to watch her step, but she won't listen to me, Orem. There will come a point when these people won't look the other way."

"Sounds risky all right."

"Not as risky as stealing a slave right off a plantation," Jamie said, turning the tables on Orem. "The details I got were very sketchy. Is it true that you have several armed men that ride with you on your slave raids? Do you have your own gang, or are they sympathizers who also feel that slavery is an abomination?"

Orem frowned. "Sorry to upset your printing press, Miss Kleg, but it was a lone man at the Diamond Head Plantation."

"I prefer Jamie to Miss Kleg, if you don't mind."

"Be a privilege, Jamie."

She was instantly back to business. "You say that you made your raid all alone?"

"I don't recall admitting that it was me. I'm not a John Brown follower. I was at the plantation the day of the escape and spoke to Colensworth about buying a slave. That's about it."

It was her turn to frown. "And what about the brutal beating of the field boss? Did you and your friends have to break his nose and jaw?"

"I told you, that man was alone. As for the field boss being beaten, I don't know all that much about it."

"Don't hand me a dish of hogwash,

Orem. I know for a fact that there was an attack on the field boss, a man named Matt Lamount. My source said that he was nearly killed."

"And you think I ought to know something about it?"

"Yes."

The innocent act wasn't doing Orem any good. He let out a long sigh and decided to face up to the attack. "The man was mistreating a young lady servant. She was planning to give some food or water to the slave who Colensworth's men had tacked up on the side of the tanning shed to die in the sun. I hit him only once."

Again, she looked at him circumspectly. It was odd to be scrutinized by a woman. It made Orem mildly uncomfortable.

"You'll excuse me if I don't see how you could have done so much damage to the man with a single punch. You aren't all that big."

"I didn't say what I hit him with, ma'am. A rifle stock does a little more damage than a fist."

A knowledgeable look came into her expression, as if she had figured out the circumstances for herself. It infected the corners of her mouth, forcing her lips to curl upward slightly.

"You might be worth another story, Orem Clancy. May I buy you a cup of coffee?"

"I'm not in the habit of letting a woman pay for such an honor. If you'd allow me, I would indeed like to sit down and talk to you for a spell."

She laughed. "Certainly, Orem. Stop by my office when you've finished here."

The judge cleared his throat. "Well, I think that we've about finished. I'll make some sort of ruling that the case has to be looked into at length. It will give you time to try to work things out with Colensworth. I don't have much hope that you'll resolve anything, but at least you'll have that much more time."

"Shall we go?" Jamie asked. "You'll be headline news in my next edition."

"I don't know if that's good. You're liable to get us both run out of town on a rail."

She laughed. It was a rich, hearty laugh. He found it quite alluring.

"Nothing ventured, nothing accomplished, Orem. The West never would have been settled if we'd been faint of heart."

"I have to wonder if we have settled anything yet. Could be that we've only stirred things up."

She laughed again. "Come on. I'm ready for that cup of coffee, and I'm eager to hear about your escapades."

"Good luck, Orem," Judge Devires said. "I think you'll be needing it."

Orem offered his arm to Jamie. She deftly shifted her pad and pencil to the opposite hand and slipped her arm through his. He could not help but feel the swell of his chest. It had been a long time since he had walked with a pretty woman. Jamie was the kind who would turn many a man's head.

His one concern about Jamie was that she did not seem to take the threats against herself or her newspaper seriously. When the slavery issue was raised, it was more than serious. It could often be deadly.

Chapter Five

*T*he wagon was sitting in the middle of
the Sabine River. Saddle-weary from three
solid days of riding, Orem rode up from the
Texas side and stopped his horse to watch.
A vaguely familiar black driver was standing knee-deep in the water, trying to figure
out how he was going to get his horse moving again. From the looks of it, the wheel
on one side had dropped into a rut. The entire carriage was tilted, and the single horse
refused to pull hard enough to get the
buggy out.

"George, are we going to be stuck here
all day?" A haughty female voice came
from inside the coach.

"Sorry, Mrs. Colensworth, but we're in
pretty deep. Old Hanna can't go forward
or back."

57

The lady stuck her head out the window and surveyed the wheel. She then spotted Orem and her face brightened with a smile.

"Hello, mister! Lend us a hand!"

He nudged Tumbleweed toward the water, but the horse balked, danced, and shied away until Orem put spurs into his ribs. Then the animal entered the shallow water, hesitant and uncertain, wading out to the wagon. Orem doffed his hat at the woman when he finally got alongside. He recognized the driver as George, the elderly servant from the Colensworth house. George didn't appear to recognize Orem, so he figured the man probably had not noticed him upon his one visit to the house.

"Howdy, ma'am. Orem Clancy, at your service. Looks like you've run amuck."

She again showed an artificial smile. She was an older woman, perhaps in her late thirties. Although there were several streaks of gray in her hair and slight wrinkles near her eyes, she was still a handsome woman. Her dress and bonnet were the latest fashion, trimmed with ribbons and lace. She was about as dandy as a little red heifer in a bed of white roses.

"We require some assistance in crossing the river." She did not ask for help. It was more of a polite demand.

Orem commenced to study the predicament, then gave his head a negative shake. "This here dun I'm riding isn't much for pulling freight, ma'am. He's barely broke to rein. If I hitched him to your buggy, he might get skittish and jerk your rig right over onto its side."

She frowned and looked over his mount. As if proving Orem's point, Tumbleweed sidestepped and pawed at the water.

"I can't just sit here in the middle of the river," she complained. "There must be some way to get out of this hole."

"Yes, ma'am. You only got to get out. Without the extra weight, your driver and I might be able to get the nag pulled free."

She noted the muddy water, then flicked an impatient glance at him. He saw the shocked, indignant look cloud her features.

"You expect me to wade to the bank in my best gown? It would ruin it!"

Orem scratched his head. "Well, you could shimmy out of the dress and splash on over to shore in your bloomers. I promise to be a gentleman and not look in your direction.''

He might have laughed at the indignant fury that came into the woman's eyes, but it would have gotten him a scalding from her tongue. To hide his amusement, he ducked his head enough that the woman could not see his smile.

She uttered a grunt of disgust under her breath and glared at Orem. "We'll manage without your help, kind sir." The sarcasm oozed from her voice. "George, come over here and carry me to shore."

Orem took a short appraisal of the black driver. He was about five and a half feet in height and must have been pushing sixty years old. If the woman had still been in baby clothes and weighed only thirty pounds, he might have managed a half-dozen steps. Considering the circumstances, she would have better odds trying to carry *him* the remainder of the way.

"Must be fifty yards to the other side," Orem pointed out. "How about I put you on my horse and lead him across?"

But Tumbleweed spooked at George's simply taking a step. He fought the bit and danced about some more, splashing and fighting the water. His eyes rolled and only Orem's soothing voice and a hand stroking his neck calmed him back down.

"It would appear to me that you haven't any control of the animal as it is," the woman said sourly. "Also, I'm not in the habit of riding astraddle. I'd as soon sit here and wait for someone else to come along before I get on that beast—with or without your help."

Orem rode his animal across to the other bank. Then he tied him off where he could munch some tall grass. He removed his gun, hitched it over the pommel of his saddle, and entered the water once more on foot. He waded out until he reached the coach, then he opened the door.

"If you'll allow me, ma'am, I'll carry you to shore. George can get around to the front of the nag and give her a jerk. If she doesn't pull out, I'll come back and lend a hand."

The woman was undecided. She looked around for more help, but Orem was the only aid in sight. With a deep sigh, she carefully edged over to the doorway.

"If you get any mud or dirty water on my dress, I'll have my husband horsewhip you."

"Is that your idea of coaxing me into being careful?"

She ignored the question. By turning her back to him and taking hold of the roof of the buggy, she got into position. He put one arm under her knees and the other up toward her shoulders. Then she let go and he was supporting her weight.

Orem was reasonably surefooted, but the river bottom was rocky in spots and the water was well above his knees. He had to take his time, carefully placing each step, then shifting his weight.

"You are undoubtedly the slowest moving man I ever met." She voiced her negative opinion of their progress.

"I haven't had much practice lugging female critters across rivers, ma'am."

She twisted to glare at him. "I'm not a female critter, I'm Roweena Colensworth, Mrs. Baldwin Colensworth! My husband is The Bull of Louisiana, owner of the Diamond Head Plantation!"

"Well now, that surely does impress me,

ma'am. What a good time I'll have at the
French Cut Saloon next time I get to
Shreveport. I can tell everyone that I was
honored to haul your carcass across the Sabine River."

She grew red in the face, eyes smoldering. "You ill-mannered, uncouth, misfit
cowboy! I insist that you make all haste to
get me across the river. I don't want you
touching me any longer than is absolutely
necessary. You stink of horseflesh!"

He took a step and let out a grunt. "You
didn't look so heav—uh, mature in the
buggy. You're a sizable woman."

She twisted in his grasp. "How dare you!
I'll—"

But her movement was poorly timed.
Orem slipped, took a step back into a soft
spot, caught himself, and tried to get his
balance. He'd have done it easily, but the
lady pushed against him with both hands.

"Don't you drop me!" she cried.

Orem swung her around to maintain his
stance and planted his foot to steady them
both. "Quit your fussing about, she-cat!
I'm in a hole!"

Mrs. Colensworth stopped struggling at

once, allowing him to again shift her weight enough to get his foot free. Then he continued to the bank without incident.

Orem set the woman down at the bank and let out a sigh of relief. He had made it without getting more than a drop or two of water on her fancy white-and-yellow gown. Her bonnet was still in perfect place on her head. He might have anticipated some grateful words for his efforts, but she lit into him with the fury of an angry hornet.

"You might have dropped me out there, you clumsy lout!"

"If that's your way of saying thank you for my help, you're welcome."

"You expect thanks!" Her voice was higher pitched now that she was safely on firm footing. "I ought to tell my husband how you insulted and manhandled me! He'd have you flogged publicly! You were enjoying holding me close out there in the water. You can't deny that!"

He shook his head. "You've been too spoiled and pampered all your life, Mrs. Colensworth. I'd as soon hold a barrel cactus as you."

"You forget your place, you boor!"

"There's no law that says I had to wade out in the middle of that river and carry you to shore. I did that out of consideration for you, since you're a lady."

"And I'm supposed to be happy about that?" She laughed with contempt. "You more than got your payment for being able to hold me so close."

Orem set his teeth, irked by her attitude. He wasn't all that fond of Colensworth, and it would seem that his wife was no improvement. Considering the stories he had heard about their son, Jace, it appeared that he'd do well to avoid the whole family.

"I'm for thinking you flatter yourself a little too much, ma'am. I'm not in the habit of taking advantage of females in distress. If it hadn't been for me, you'd have landed right in the middle of the river."

"That's utterly preposterous! I would never end up sitting in the middle of a river. I'm a Colensworth, not some pig farmer's wife!"

Orem put his hands on his hips, provoked at the high-handed attitude of this woman. Up to that point, he had not discovered one single thing he liked about Colensworth, his son, or his wife.

"A name doesn't stop accidents, ma'am. I'm also thinking it sure doesn't make you a nice person, either."

That put some color in her already rubicund cheeks. "Climb on your horse and ride off, cowboy. Be thankful that I don't insist on having you whipped for daring to insult me and lay your hands on me."

Orem should have walked away without a backward glance. Instead, he took a step toward the woman, making her move back from him. He put hard eyes on her and pressed forward a second step.

"I wouldn't attempt to lay hands on a woman who was old enough to be my mother. You could use a lesson in manners, ma'am. If I wasn't a gentleman, and twenty years your junior, I'd be right proud to give you one."

She straightened her shoulders suddenly and planted her feet. "How dare you, you . . . you boor!" She snapped off the words and swung an open palm at his face.

Orem had been in fights a number of

times, so he instinctively ducked the slap.
Things got out of hand after that.

The woman had put a lot into her swing.
When she missed, she took a full step back.
Her foot sank into the water at the river-
bank and she instantly tried to shift her
weight and pull back. Orem came out of
his stoop and reached out to catch her. The
result was not much of a success. He got
only a handful of her gown at the sleeve.
It ripped away as she turned completely
around and sat down with a plop in about
six inches of river mud and water.

"No!" she screamed, holding up both
hands in dismay. "Not my new dress!"

Orem quickly took hold of her wrists to
pull her up out of the shallow water. No
sooner was she on her feet than she started
swinging at him with both fists. He had to
back away with his hands up to ward her
off.

"Calm down!" He tried to quiet her as
he dodged another onslaught. "It was an
accident!"

"An accident, my foot! You did that on
purpose!" she cried, looking around for a

weapon. "You knocked me down in the water! You vile, dirty, stinking cowhand!"

Orem was as good with his gun or fists as most, but he knew when he was overmatched. When Mrs. Colensworth leaned over to pick up a broken tree branch, he grabbed his horse and swung into the saddle. He charged on down the trail at full tilt, with the woman's curses still in his ears.

After a quarter-mile run, he slowed the dun and looked over his shoulder. The carriage and woman were both lost to sight. He emitted a low whistle and patted his horse on the neck.

Pointing his mount for Blackwater, Orem spoke aloud to the dun. "We're doing real well with the Colensworth family, Tumbleweed. I steal a slave from the old man and help his wife take a dunk in the river. I'm not scared of Baldwin Colensworth, but I sure hope that we never lock horns with that wife of his again!"

Chapter Six

*M*rs. Colensworth held up the laundered dress and looked at it with open disapproval. The sleeve was torn right off. The muddy water had left discolored patches that washing had not removed. Her best dress was ruined.

"It was such a fine dress, mistress." Sarah shook her head, trying to put a degree of sympathy in her voice. "What a shame that it's ruined."

"I know. It was brand-new."

"Mister George said it was some cowboy's fault."

She looked hard at her maid. "Is that what he really said, Sarah?"

The servant girl was basically honest. Even at eighteen years of age, she had never learned how to lie very well.

"Well, he did say that it was partly an accident."

Mrs. Colensworth frowned. "I thought that's what he would say. I should never have let that smelly cowboy carry me across the river. He was about the rudest man I ever met."

"George said he had seen the man before, but he couldn't remember where."

The woman grimaced at the dress once more. "George's memory isn't what it used to be. I sometimes wonder that he remembers to get up in the morning."

"Yes, mistress."

"And what about this episode with Togg? Who would dare to come right into our yard and steal one of our slaves?"

Sarah swallowed hard and hid her eyes from her mistress. "I couldn't see the man in the dark. It could have been anyone."

Mrs. Colensworth let out a sigh and tossed the dress into a box. "Did you hear the man's voice? Did you see what he was wearing? I've been told only that Matt was hit in the face with a club and your beau is gone. What started it all? Did Togg try to run off to Mexico?"

Sarah felt her face burn at the reference to Togg as her beau. "That's what he told me, mistress. Togg almost reached the river before Matt and the others caught up with him and brought him back. Master Colensworth let them string Togg up to the tanning shed. I think he would have died there."

Roweena gave a sweep with her hand. "I would have intervened, Sarah, if I'd been here. The beating was something Togg deserved, but to hang him up to die under the sun is a waste. It's too hard to get decent workers these days. There hasn't been a slave auction since Lincoln took office." She looked directly at Sarah. There was something sinister and ruthless about the expression. When she spoke, her voice masked the wickedness in her eyes. "I can't believe that Togg would leave you behind, Sarah. I told you that there was a good chance the two of you might be paired off together."

Sarah ducked her head. "We wanted to be married proper, mistress."

The woman thought for a moment, then nodded. "Yes, I remember you asked me something about a ceremony." She let out a cynical grunt. "But you won't be seeing him again now. Togg will run forever."

"One of the local drummers said that he'd seen Togg at some man's ranch—the one who came to the plantation and tried to buy Togg."

Roweena considered that bit of news. "Maybe his showing up at that ranch is more than a coincidence, Sarah. I'll bet that the fellow who tried to buy Togg came back and stole him later that same night. Do you happen to know the name of this strange character?"

"Yes, mistress. His name is Orem Clancy."

If Mrs. Colensworth had been wearing wooden teeth, they would have dropped to the floor. "Orem Clancy! Orem Clancy!" She struggled to find words, but she couldn't. She kicked the box that held her gown, she knocked over the stool at her dressing table, she grabbed the pillow from her bed and punched it.

"No! No! No!" she cried. "It can't be true! It can't!"

"I'm sure that was his name, mistress."

"It's also the name of the man who carried me across the Sabine River! That man is rolling up a score that Baldwin will soon settle!" She cursed Orem loud and long. "Blast his rotten hide! Baldwin had better get even for this. I hope he has that man strung up by his thumbs!"

Sarah didn't reply to that, but she silently vowed to give a special thanks in her nightly prayers for Orem Clancy. No one in Louisiana had dared to stand up to Baldwin Colensworth, not until now. Orem Clancy would need a lot of help. Turning to her work, she decided she also would ask that somehow, someday, she and Togg would be together.

The door to Orem's office opened. It was his main assistant, the man who managed the bank in his absence. He had a curious look of disapproval on his face.

"Yes, Johnson?"

"There's a young woman to see you, Mr. Clancy. She . . . well, she says that she is a newspaper publisher and that you met her in Shreveport."

"I remember. Send her in."

Johnson frowned and took a deep breath. "She isn't exactly decent, Mr. Clancy. There is . . . I mean, someone has. . . ." He struggled to find the right words, then blurted it out. "I believe she has been tarred and feathered."

Orem came out of his chair as quickly as if he had sat on an angry rattlesnake. "What?"

"Yes. I told her to wait outside. It wouldn't do to have anyone in town thinking that our bank would cater to such . . . such a scraggly looking individual."

Orem darted past Johnson at a run. He reached the front of the bank to see a crowd gathered. The center of their attention was Jamie Kleg. At least Orem assumed it was the woman Judge Devires had introduced to him. From her dreadful appearance, it was hard to tell who was under the dried black tar and thousands of bits of feathers.

"Miss Kleg?" he ventured, pushing past several spectators to get within speaking distance of the woman. "Jamie, is that you?"

Within the blackened face, Jamie's eyes

were red and filled with tears. Her hair was a mat of thick, black tar. Her ragged dress was coated with grime and a multitude of white and brown chicken feathers. She opened her mouth to speak, but there were no words at her command.

"Brought her in on the stage." A man spoke up from the group of people. "Hope she didn't make a mess of the coach."

Orem moved quickly to her side. He took hold of her wrist and pushed through the gathering throng of curious people. No one blocked his path, for he was known and respected in Blackwater. However, a considerable number of onlookers followed after them.

"What'd she do?" someone asked.

"Must be some bar girl they ran out of town!" a woman judged in an indignant tone of voice.

"How come the banker took up with her?" another man wondered aloud.

"You think he knows her?" a second woman asked.

Orem shut out the dozens of questions. He strode as fast as Jamie could manage.

Then, reaching the hotel, he went in and closed the door behind them.

The owner of the hotel was Jim James, a man Orem had helped to start his business. Jim was about the same age as Orem, but shorter and somewhat better looking. He stared open-mouthed, seeing the condition of the woman.

"I knew you were hard up for female companionship, Orem. Is this what you have to resort to just to get one to be seen with you?"

Orem didn't find any humor in his words. His voice was stern and brisk. "I need a room for her right now, Jim!"

Jim looked past Orem to the crowd of people. He didn't hesitate, but reached for the keys on the wall behind him.

"Let's put her next to your room."

Orem led Jamie past the counter and down the hall. He stopped long enough for Jim to open a door, then took her into the room. Only after closing the door did he take a breath and let go of her.

Jim observed her from head to foot. "That tar won't come off, Orem. Even with a pile of scrubbing, she'll be black for a month. I don't think it'll come out of her hair at all. It'll have to grow out."

"Get some lantern oil, Jim. I used some of that once to remove tar."

"Right away, Orem. I think you'll be needing a couple of gallons."

As soon as they were alone, Orem took inventory of the young woman. Her face and arms were smeared with dried black tar. Her clothes had been torn in spots and she wore only one shoe. She had feathers glued to her clothes and her hair from the tar. Her eyes were red from crying and her lip was swollen from a blow. She was about as pitiful as any person Orem had ever seen.

"I'm not a betting man, but I would lay odds that I know how you ended up looking this way."

She looked around slowly, as if trying to decide whether to sit down. She decided against the idea, probably thinking that the tar would stick to the bedding.

"They broke up the printing press. They . . . they burned all my books and papers . . . all my personal belongings . . . everything!"

"If I recall, the judge warned you to stop writing about slavery. You live in a very strong slave state, and feelings are running high against Lincoln and the North."

"The First Amendment gives us the right to tell the truth."

"It doesn't give you any protection from those who disagree with you," he pointed out. "How'd you end up here?"

She rubbed her hands together, trying to get the tar off. It was a wasted effort.

"I wrote about some of the atrocities being inflicted upon the slaves—the beatings, a death or two, the mating of them like animals. It was supposed to be a sympathetic look at the plight of the slaves. You might guess that it wasn't well received.

"The paper hadn't been on the streets an hour when a horde of people came storming into my office. They grabbed me and dragged me out into the street. Several of the women had buckets of hot tar." She paused and fingered the tender spot on her lip. "They about scalded me."

"Then someone emptied a sack of feathers over your head," Orem guessed.

"Yes. They were all laughing and shouting vile names at me. I was pushed and shoved about, and one of the women hit me in the face. She called me a slave-loving troublemaker."

"How'd you end up on the stage?"

"They stuck me on a child's wagon and I was pulled out of town about a mile. When they turned me loose, I was told not to come back. If I did, they said the next time they would do the job right and boil me in oil."

"The driver found you walking along the road?"

"He wasn't going to stop. I blocked the trail, and the team about ran right over me." She sighed. "He didn't want me in his coach, but he finally put down a tarp and let me sit on the floor. I bounced around all the way here. I remembered Judge Devires saying that you had the bank in Blackwater, and. . . ." She lifted her shoulders in a shrug.

"I'll see about getting you something to wear."

"What about this tar?"

"The lantern oil ought to break down

some of the tar. Jim will bring you a bath-tub and the strongest soap he can find. Maybe you can get most of it off."

Jamie looked into the small mirror that was placed above the room's only table and washbowl. She groaned, seeing the horrid reflection, and turned quickly away.

"Am I going to cause trouble for you, Orem? I—I didn't know where else to turn."

"Don't worry, Jamie. Everyone thinks of me as a rebel here in Blackwater, but I've got some friends too." He grinned. "Besides, you don't look any worse than some of the other girls I've been seen with."

Jim entered the room again. He had a can with him. "I brought some rags. You can soak them in oil and then try to wash or rinse the tar loose."

"She'll need a bath too."

Jim smiled. "Not for at least an hour. I'll bet it takes that long to shed that coat of feathers and tar."

"Do you want someone to help?" Orem offered. "I could send one of my women tellers over."

"No, I'll manage."

"Then we'll leave you to your task."

Jamie's face showed her gratitude. "Thank you, Orem. I—I don't know what would have happened to me if you hadn't been here."

"I'll see if I can find something for you to wear." He grinned. "I wonder what goes good with black?"

"Keep the color dark," she agreed, smiling slightly. "I don't think I'll ever get all this tar off."

Orem gave Jim a shove out the door and followed him into the hallway. Once away from her room, Jim took hold of his arm.

"What happened? Who is she?"

"Her name is Jamie Kleg. She operated a newspaper in Shreveport. Suffice it to say she printed one too many antislavery articles. People are getting a mite testy about that right now."

"Speaking of which, you aren't still going to pay Baldwin Colensworth a visit, are you?"

"I've got to make him an offer for the slave that I've got in Texas. I'll tell him that I found the man on the Texas side of the Sabine River."

"He won't believe that."

"It doesn't matter what he believes. I spoke to Judge Devires up in Shreveport. He's giving me time to get this sorted out. If I don't, I'll be an open target for any thug in the state. I want to get Colensworth paid off so I don't have to worry about a price on the slave's head, or mine, either. Baldwin isn't the kind of man who likes to get stepped on."

"Jace was in town while you were up in Shreveport. He had a bully tear apart some guy for saying something against slavery. It's getting to be a real touchy subject all over the South, Orem."

"War is coming, Jim. No one's going to stop it. There's been a lot of killing already, and it's going to get worse."

"Which side are you going to fight for?"

"It might be impossible, but I'm going to try to remain neutral."

Jim laughed at that idea. "You've been buying and freeing slaves for years. Now you tell me that you're going to be neutral?"

"Each of those men has repaid me for the price I spent to acquire him. I see the price I paid for those men as indentures, not a sign of ownership."

"Well, I think your lady friend in there demonstrated the need for being discreet about your feelings on slavery. When people dare to tar and feather a young woman, war can't be very far off in the future."

"I'm afraid you're right about that, Jim. Lincoln will declare all men free one day soon, then it'll be up to the North to enforce that decree. Painful as it is to think about it, war is coming."

Chapter Seven

*T*ogg held the rifle up and aimed down the barrel. He had never fired a gun—had never even held one in his hands before.

"See the target," Kip Jones instructed. "Put it in your sights, hold your breath, and squeeze the trigger."

The rifle butt bucked against Togg's shoulder. He blinked from the blast of the gun and lost sight of his target. The result was another miss.

"You did it again, Togg!" Kip was losing patience. "Don't jerk the trigger, squeeze it. If you're expecting the gun to go off, you'll pull your shot."

"Well, I know it's going to go off," Togg explained. "How can I pull the trigger and not think the gun is going to fire?"

"That ain't the idea. You squeeze the

85

shot off. You keep your eye on the target and pull the trigger slowly. When it goes off, you should be able to see the bullet hit. You got to learn not to be afraid of the noise. Watch how Henry does it this time."

Togg concentrated on Henry. He was the youngest of the three of them, but he was good with a gun. He took up a stance, aimed, and fired all in one motion. The result was a hole through the wooden slab, right inside the circle they had drawn with a piece of charcoal.

"See that?" Kip was at him again. "See how he didn't flinch?"

Togg loaded his rifle again and raised it. He aligned the sights again, steadying the barrel with his left hand. As he found the target, he stopped breathing. Then he tried to pull the trigger back very slowly.

The gun went off as if by accident. This time his bullet went into the board. It was almost as close as the one Henry had fired.

"You did it!" Kip cried. "You nailed it right square in the middle!"

Togg was all smiles. "Yeah! I see what you mean, Kip. This ain't all that hard to do."

"Practice is what it takes," Henry said. "We've been shooting for several months. You looked like a hunter with that last shot."

Togg put his attention on the two black men. They spoke with confidence, not mumbling or shuffling over their words like a field slave. These two were learning to be free men.

"What're you men going to do, once you've paid your debt to Master Clancy?" he asked them.

Kip laughed at the question and Henry shook his head. "How many times we got to tell you, Togg? Orem Clancy ain't our master. He's our boss—same as if we were white men. We work for him, that's all."

But that seemed so farfetched that Togg couldn't really understand it. They were working for wages, paying off a debt. Once that debt was paid, these men were free to go where they wished. What a tremendous feeling!

"All right. But what will you do, once you pay your dues?"

"We ain't sure, Togg. We have a responsibility to other slaves. We got to help in any way we can."

"Here in Texas?"

Kip sighed. "No. Too many people are hot about the slavery issue here. We could end up dead real sudden, staying here."

"Then what?"

"They need wranglers up in Wyoming. They're laying tracks for the railroad in Kansas and farther east, and up in Colorado and Nevada, they're hiring miners. We'll find us some honest work all right. We'll set a good example and make people see that we're no different than they are."

Togg wrestled with the idea. "How can you know which is right? How do you decide without being told?"

Kip scowled. "No one tells us where to go or what to do any longer, Togg. We're free to go where we please. So long as we obey the law, we can do anything we want. That's what freedom is all about. You got to stop thinking like a field slave."

Togg felt his chest expand. He felt a surge of jubilation. "I'll be a free man. All I got to do is pay my debt to Master . . . Mr. Orem Clancy."

Henry didn't speak much but he showed one of his rare grins. "So what is in your mind to do first, Togg?"

"Yeah," Kip joined in. "What do you want to do next?"

Togg didn't hesitate. "The first thing I want is my Sarah. She's the prettiest girl in all the world to me."

"Sarah?" Kip repeated the name. "Where is she at?"

"On the Diamond Head. She's a servant in the house."

Kip let out a low whistle. "When you pick a hard tree to climb, you don't worry about how high the branches are, do you?"

"I love that woman," Togg declared. "And I'll have her as my wife."

"The Bull of Louisiana might have something to say about that. I don't think Orem can buy someone like her."

"Then I'll buy her. If I have to work twenty-four hours a day for the next ten years, I'll get her away from that plantation."

"Well, good luck," Kip told him evenly. "You'll need it."

Togg could see the skepticism in the

faces of his newfound friends. Here was an untrained field slave, boasting about what he was going to do. He was a man who didn't know the meaning of the word "freedom," and he talked of taking his girl from the clutches of one of the most powerful men in the state of Louisiana.

Still, the feelings were burning in Togg's chest. He knew that there had to be a way to get the woman he loved. He could visualize her sparkling brown eyes, the smooth, soft skin, the sensuous lips that would part in one of her timid smiles. She was a treasure beyond worth. With Orem's guidance and the help of men like Kip and Henry, he would learn to be a free man. Then he would find a way to get his Sarah. He had to believe that. There was a way. There had to be a way.

Orem went to the room twice, but Jamie refused to let him in. On his second trip, he and Jim took a tub of hot water to her door. She opened it enough to allow them to slide it inside, then quickly closed it in their faces.

"I'd say the lantern oil isn't working too

well," Jim ventured. "I once saw a man who had been tarred and feathered. It stuck on his skin for close to a month. He had to shave his head to get the stuff out of his hair too. I wonder if your friend will have to cut her hair off."

"I hope not."

"You get her something to wear?"

"Yeah. I'll relax in my room until she gets nerve enough to call me. She can't stay hidden away forever."

"I'll be out front if you need me for anything."

"Thanks, Jim."

"Sure," he said with a grin. "I'll put her room, the bath, and all the extras on your bill."

"Thanks a lot!"

Orem stopped at the lady's room and listened. He was unable to tell if she was groaning or crying. Either way, it was not a happy sound on the other side of the door.

"I'll be right next door to you, Jamie. When you're dressed, just knock on the wall."

"Wait a minute, Orem." Her voice stopped him.

He stood there for a moment and heard the splashing of water. It came as a surprise to have her open the door. She was wrapped in a blanket, covering everything but her throat and head.

"I . . . I feel like the worst kind of. . . ."

"What can I do to help?" He tried to make it easy for her.

One hand appeared out from under the blanket. Jamie put it to her hair and pulled a glob until it stood straight up.

"I can't see what I'm doing. Would you see if you can get some of this stuff out of my hair?"

"I'm not very handy at—"

"Please," she murmured softly. "I . . . I don't want some stranger in here with me. It'll take me only a minute to wrap something around me. Besides, I know that you're a gentleman."

"Being a gentleman won't help with that tar," he said as compassionately as he could. He took a closer inspection of her hair. "If that stuff won't dissolve with the lantern oil, it'll have to be cut."

She let out a deep sigh. "Bring a pair of scissors with you. I've got to be rid of this black tar!"

Orem rounded up a pair of scissors and went to work on Jamie's hair. It was not a pretty affair. The tar would not separate from the strands of hair. He rubbed and he worked it between his hands, but the end result was always the same. He had to cut the matted knots away. By the time he had finished, the poor woman resembled a scalded cat.

"I don't know what we can do about your remaining hair, Jamie. You'll have to wear a bonnet or something."

She let out another long sigh of resignation. "Just cut it all to make it an even length. I'll manage with whatever is left."

"But, Jamie, I cut hair like a butcher. I'm making a mess of this."

"You can't make a mess out of a mess, Orem. Please cut it for me."

He did as she asked, severing the ends until her hair was no longer than his own. Soon her head was free of tar, except for the smudges on her face.

"This blasted stuff seems to become part

of the skin. I used that smelly oil and then soap over and over. I can't begin to get clean," she said sadly.

"I'm afraid that some of that will have to wear off."

She looked up at him. She was ashamed of her appearance, but she still had fire in her eyes. No one could dampen her spirit.

"They did this to me for telling the truth, Orem. Those wretched people are so narrowminded about slavery that they couldn't stand to hear it."

"I've run into that on occasion."

"Look at me! I must be the most ugly woman on earth!"

He did look. In fact, he took a long, hard look at her. She had black smears on both cheeks and a smudge on her forehead, but otherwise she had gotten most of the tar off her face. Her hair was wet and very short, but her gray-blue eyes were inviting. When she pursed her lips in a tight frown, he found her remarkably enchanting.

"I think that you're the prettiest woman I ever laid eyes on, Jamie."

"Don't be ridiculous, Orem! I never. . . ." Her eyes locked with his. "I mean, you are being flattering to make me feel better, because you are . . . a gentleman." A dreamy sort of expression entered her eyes. "I can't imagine anyone—"

Unable to stop himself, Orem leaned forward and kissed her. The act must have shocked Jamie, as she did not even draw back away from him. Instead, she seemed to allow him to linger.

Her eyes were still closed when he regained his senses and pulled back from her. He couldn't get his mental faculties to work. He was trying to think of something to say, when she smiled at him.

"That was very sweet of you, Orem." Her voice was soft and gentle. "But I'm all right. I'm not the kind of woman to feel sorry for myself."

He found that his heart was pounding like a stampede. "I wasn't being all that considerate, Jamie. I kind of lost my head for a moment."

That put a slight smile on her lips. "Sure, I'm so irresistible right now."

"My thinking exactly."

She laughed lightly. "You're nice, Orem. I can almost believe you."

"How about getting dressed? I'll take you over to the café for something to eat."

That got her to thinking again. She turned away from him and looked at her reflection in the mirror. "How do I hide my head? I look like I've been scalped by bloodthirsty Indians."

He retrieved the package of things he'd found for her. The dress was a dull black—not very pretty—and he had gotten her two scarves and a gray poke bonnet.

"You do the best you can," he told her. "That's all a body can do. As long as I'm with you, no one is going to laugh at you."

She smiled and pushed him toward the door. "You can wait out in the hall while I get dressed. If you aren't ashamed to be seen with me, I shouldn't be bashful about going to dinner with you."

Orem went out of the room and leaned against the wall. He knew that Jamie was a special kind of woman. She was brave and stubborn. Being run out of town for her view on the treatment of slaves wouldn't slow her down. When the war came, she would be outspoken against slave owners. That was a dangerous position to take. If she had been a man, she would have been tarred and feathered for real—not given a symbolic dousing. Hot tar burned on contact and melded with the skin. The feathers implanted themselves right under the top layer of tar and adhered to the flesh. It was a brutal, vicious thing to do to anyone. Jamie had been lucky this time. But what would happen if she started up again?

Chapter Eight

*J*ace Colensworth paused while cleaning his pistol. He had been listening to Roweena and Baldwin. The subject was one that held some interest for him.

"I rode up to Kanterville while I was on the Texas side of the Sabine," Jace told them both. "Orem Clancy has a new slave—Togg Jackson."

"Then he has our slave working for him!" Baldwin was visibly upset.

"I talked to a few people around that part of the country, Pa. It seems that Orem Clancy doesn't have any slaves. He hires black workers like they were white. He pays them money and lets them earn their freedom. From what I could find out, he's been doing it for a number of years. So far, he's freed near a dozen black men."

99

"I don't understand that man." Colensworth uttered a mild oath. "He doesn't have good sense. We can't be letting these black people run free. If they get to thinking they don't need us, we'll have a revolt on every plantation in the country. There will be a war between whites and blacks!"

"He's a crude, vulgar troublemaker," Roweena said. "He called me names and pushed me into the river. That man needs to be horsewhipped. He needs to be taught a lesson."

"What do you say, Pa? Want me to take Lars into Blackwater and show the banker that we mean business?"

Colensworth thought for a moment. "He needs a lesson, but I haven't decided what kind of lesson. Judge Devires informed me that I couldn't press charges against him until there was some proof that he helped Togg escape. Harboring a runaway slave is not much of a crime."

Jace ran his hand over the smooth barrel of his pistol. "You want me to get some proof that he stole Togg?"

"Like what?" Roweena asked.

"I'll slip over to his place and get an admission from Togg. I could bring him back, if you want."

"That sounds like a good plan to me, Baldwin," Roweena said. "What do you think?"

"Don't you get into any trouble, Jace. If you can't get him back without a fight, leave him. We'll find another way to get even with the banker from Blackwater."

"Sure, Pa. I'll be careful."

"Take Lars, then. If you run into trouble, he's about the most able man on the place."

Jace grinned. "We'll head out at first light. We ought to be back in two or three days."

"If you cross trails with Orem," Roweena told her son firmly, "don't forget that he insulted your mother."

A wicked light danced in Jace's eyes. "I'll square that debt for you, Mother. Orem Clancy is going to regret his actions. I won't rest until he has paid for what he did to you."

She smiled. "You're a good boy, Jace."

"I'll find Lars and get him started to packing. When I come back, Togg will be in chains." He grinned. "Maybe the banker will be too."

Jim James shook his head slowly, a genuine look of concern shining on his face.

"It's like walking into a bear cave to wake up a slumbering grizzly, Orem. Colensworth will probably have you beaten to death for setting foot on his property."

"As long as Togg is listed as a runaway slave, he can never be a free man. I'll make Colensworth a decent offer. What would he have to gain by not accepting payment?"

"The payment he'll want is your hide. Let someone else ride out with the offer. At the very least, take someone with you. I'd hate to see you drawn and quartered."

Jamie entered to hear the last words. She frowned at Orem and looked at Jim for an explanation. Her hand went up to make certain her scarf was in place. With the long-sleeved dress, there was little visible evidence of her tarring and feathering.

"Did you say that someone wanted Orem's hide?"

"He's going up to the Diamond Head Plantation. The Bull of Louisiana will skin him alive."

Jamie's eyes lit up with alarm. "What are you thinking of, Orem? Why should you risk your life to see such a man?"

"I owe him for a slave, Jamie. Until I get the papers on Togg, he'll be a wanted man. If he ever returns to the plantation, he'll be killed."

She rubbed her hands together, absently working to remove some of the black from the skin along her knuckles. The tar was slow to dissolve.

"There has to be another way. I know something of Baldwin Colensworth from my research. He wields a lot of power with the other plantation owners. He once showed up in Shreveport to speak at a pro-slavery gathering. I believe his wife also met with the governor once on the subject of slavery. She's very outspoken."

"I've encountered her once myself," Orem admitted, recalling the incident at the river crossing. "I would rather tackle a grizzly barehanded than face her again. But this has to be settled. They're powerful in Louisiana all right, but they can't get at Togg in Texas. I have to try to right the books."

"The money you can afford to offer for that slave won't be enough to make any difference to Colensworth," Jim pointed out. "He's going to want you to pay physically for embarrassing him. I think you're crazy to even think of going up there."

But Orem was steadfast. "I can't avoid the man forever. If he won't listen to reason, I'll try and get Judge Devires to intervene. There might be some way to protect Togg legally."

Jamie stood boldly in front of Orem, as if to block him from leaving. "The war is coming," she said with certainty. "It would be the act of a blasted fool to get killed trying to save one slave. Lincoln will soon declare them all free men."

Orem let out a long sigh, knowing he would have to tell them both the truth. He didn't like the idea of worrying Jamie, for she was still recovering from the shock of losing everything she owned. He was her one hope to start over, to borrow money and start another newspaper. However, it was not in his nature to tell lies to his friends.

"There is a price on my head," he told them bluntly. "Colensworth has posted a reward for my hide."

"What?" Jim was appalled.

"No!" Jamie cried. "He can't do that!"

Orem held up his hands to silence them both. "You can see why I have to go face him. I've got to clear this up before someone with a gun tries to collect the reward."

"When did you learn of this?" Jim wanted to know.

"One of the customers mentioned it to me. I asked around and learned that the rumor was true. I'm worth five hundred dollars . . . dead."

"All the more reason for not going to that plantation!" Jamie objected. "You'll be playing right into Colensworth's hands!"

"I'll sneak in and speak to him personally. So long as I avoid his hired men, I can handle him."

"And supposing you get caught?"

Orem shrugged. "Then I'll be roasted alive."

"I'll go with you," Jamie suggested. "He won't dare do anything while you have a news reporter with you. I could write him out of Louisiana if he harmed you."

"The press isn't all that powerful here, or didn't you find that out at Shreveport? Your being a newspaperwoman didn't stop them from tarring and feathering you."

"But—"

Orem again held up his hand. "I'll be careful," he told them both as he went out into the bright afternoon sun.

Even as he walked to the stable, he had no misgivings about his plan to try to reason with Colensworth. The man was not the kind to back down. His only hope was that he could somehow get him to relent enough to name a price for Togg. If he could not be reasoned with, then Orem's next recourse was to go to Judge Devires and try to get some kind of order to protect himself.

Jamie had watched Orem ride out of town several hours before. Now she remained in the shadows, keeping out of sight. She tucked in the bulky shirt and hitched up the breeches.

"How do men stand to be confined in these tight pants?" she asked Jim aloud. "Can't walk or bend. It's like wrapping canvas around your legs!"

Jim shook his head, concern in his eyes.

"If Orem doesn't end up killed, he'll likely kill me for not stopping you. I don't like the idea of your dressing up like a man. What if something happens to you?"

With her short hair, Jamie was able to don a man's clothing and pass herself off as a man—from a distance. Up close, her face would give her away. She had delicate features and a very feminine voice. Jim had given her the clothes, but he was not convinced that she was doing the right thing. To be seen in such an outfit could get her tarred and feathered again.

"You just point me toward Orem's ranch. He's got to have some help, in case something does go wrong with his scheme."

Jim had drawn a map on a sheet of paper. He still was not in favor of the idea but he passed it to her. "Stick to the main trail until you cross the Sabine River. Then bear off toward the tall peaks. Once you get onto his land, you'll be able to follow the beaten path to his house."

She mounted the horse, raised a hand in farewell, and rode through the back streets of town. Then she picked up the main road and turned toward the Texas border.

The sun was hot and Jamie had not thought to bring any food. She did have a canteen, so the water would have to hold her until she reached Orem's ranch.

It was an odd feeling to follow a man into danger. Jamie had been a natural snooper all her life. Even as a little girl, she had been nosy and inquisitive. She had enjoyed reading and had learned to write at an early age. Long before being able to strike out on her own, she had wanted to write for a newspaper. The jobs offered her were not very exciting. One newspaper wanted her to solicit recipes and report on the local gossip. Another offered her a position writing the women's news, information about fundraising, new babies, birthdays, party announcements, and the like.

It would have been about as exciting as covering a knitting bee.

No, Jamie had wanted to report the major events. She wanted to make a difference. Her desire to get involved had been a consuming passion. It had gotten her tarred and feathered. She could not sit back and simply report the news, she had to express her own point of view as well. Her editorial columns had made her less than popular.

Depression washed over her at the memory of her press and little shop. She had worked so hard to get started. Every dime she had earned had gone back into her business. It was all lost now. The people of the town had destroyed her work and her dreams. They had burned everything she owned. It would be very hard to go back to writing news. Their actions had broken her spirit.

In all her wildest dreams, she had never considered being subjected to the abuse and humiliation of being covered with tar and feathers. How could people be so cruel? She had only reported her own true findings. She had not made up any lies or stories about the suffering of the slaves. The words written were documented proof that slavery was immoral and brutal.

The people in the town of Shreveport had not been condemned in her paper, only the owners of the slaves. Most people didn't have slaves. It was the plantation owners who bought and sold people. Why had the local people reacted so violently?

Jamie had an inkling about the attitude of the town's populace. Telling someone else that what they were doing was wrong usually got a hostile rebuttal. No one cared to hear that he was immoral and wrong about an issue. To maintain their own peace of mind, people were forced to defend themselves. In Jamie's case, that had meant getting rid of the conscience they did not want. The attack on her was a way of bolstering their own position. When all was said and done about the slavery issue, Jamie decided that she would not be needed as the conscience of an entire town.

She brought her thoughts back to the present and Orem, who was already on his way to Diamond Head. He was a man with a sense of justice, a man who lived by a code of honor. He was risking his life to try to gain Togg's papers. With a price on his head, he had to face Colensworth. There had to be a way to resolve the slave's position without bloodshed. But that was not The Bull of Louisiana's reputation. He was hard, ruthless, and tough. Dealing with him would be next to impossible.

She started thinking about something else. Orem had been very helpful during her time of need. He had shown her a kind and gentle nature that touched her deeply. How could she ever repay him for taking her in and helping her?

She remembered the way he had kissed her. It had been impulsive, as if they were both drawn to each other. At first, she had thought that he was only being sweet. He might have felt that she needed reassurance and support and wanted to demonstrate to her that she was still desirable. But he claimed that he had kissed her for his own gratification, as if he was drawn irresistibly to her. That warmed her more than the heat from the merciless sun.

Since that singular episode, he'd been the perfect gentleman. But she could see something in the depths of his eyes. He would often gaze at her, his eyes filled with longing. Was there a chance that Orem was in love with her?

She almost giggled like a schoolgirl at the thought. Wouldn't that be something—Orem Clancy in love with a tar-covered woman!

Chapter Nine

*O*rem skirted the cotton fields and stuck to a row of trees, which had been planted for a windbreak. It was no easy task to reach the plantation house without being seen. He had to leave his horse tied behind the tack shed, then slip carefully along a corral fence to the back of the barn. It was dusk, so he waited and watched from that position.

The field boss, Matt Lamount, brought in the field slaves a few minutes after the sun went down. They were allowed to go to their huts for the evening. Then a couple of men rounded up horses and left. Orem could only guess that they were off to town for an evening of entertainment. As it was Saturday, that would be logical.

Roweena came out of the house with the

pretty young black girl whom Orem had seen on his previous visit. She was instructing the girl on how to clean a fine-looking rug. Old George appeared a few minutes later and informed the lady of the house that supper was ready.

"Do it the way I told you, Sarah," Roweena Colensworth told the young woman sternly. "If you damage my favorite carpet, I'll have it taken out of your hide. You hear me?"

"Yes, mistress." Sarah was quick with her response. "I'll be very careful."

Turning to George, Roweena looked at her hands. "Inform Master Baldwin that I'll be along just as soon as I wash this dirt off. I detest doing chores that should be readily handled by servants."

"Yes, ma'am, I'll tell the master."

Orem waited until Sarah was alone. She carefully beat the rug and shook the dirt from the thick carpet. She was so engrossed in her work, she didn't notice him until he was next to her. When she recognized him, she put a hand to her mouth to stifle a cry of surprise.

"Oh, no!" she said in a hushed voice.

"Whatever are you doing here? Master Baldwin will skin you alive!"

Orem gave her a tight grin. "I hope it won't come to that."

"You shouldn't be here," she whispered. "Why did you risk coming back?"

"Togg is listed as a runaway slave, and Baldwin Colensworth put a price on my head. I've got to get those two items cleared away. The only way to do that is speak to the man himself."

"He won't listen to you, Mr. Clancy. He wants you dead."

"How many people are still about?" He returned to business. "I saw a couple of men leave a few minutes ago."

"Clay and Matt are around someplace, but I don't know just where. Clay often checks the slave quarters after dark. He has the tracker dogs and is in charge of security. No one messes with Clay."

"How about in the house? Who all is inside?"

"Just Mr. and Mrs. Colensworth. They're in the dining room."

Orem took a deep breath, wishing he could speak to Colensworth alone. Roweena was likely to be harder to reason with than the old man himself. She had shown a mean temper and a scathing tongue. Orem didn't know a whole lot about women but he knew that some of them had to get even for a humiliation. Roweena blamed him for the ruin of her fine dress. That could be more of a liability than having Colensworth up in arms because Orem had dared to steal one of his slaves.

"Excuse me, Mr. Clancy, but I was wondering about Togg. Is he all right?"

Even the shadows of the night could not hide the sparkle in Sarah's eyes. Orem didn't doubt that the young lady was being more straightforward than she had ever been in her life.

"I don't get to spend much time at the ranch, but Togg has two fine men to teach him a trade," Orem said. "On my last trip up to my place, he was talking everyone's ear off about how he was going to take you away from Diamond Head."

She shook her head, but there was a tender smile on her lips. "I wonder if that man will ever grow up and think with his head."

"If this works out, maybe there will

come a day when the two of you can be together."

"That would take a war. George says there might be a real war coming. I don't think I'd like that."

"Freedom has a high price, Sarah. We fought a war so that we could be free of England. We fought the Mexicans to make Texas a free state, and I guess it'll take another fight to ensure that no man is a slave."

"And you're willing to die for that," she stated simply. "What a decent man you are, Mr. Clancy."

He had no reply to that. As far as he could determine, he was acting in the only honorable way. When a price was put on a man's head, he would do anything to get that price removed.

"I've got to go, Sarah. I don't dare put off talking to Colensworth longer than necessary. If some of his men should show up, I'd be hanging on that tack shed come morning."

"Be careful, Mr. Clancy."

He touched the brim of his hat and slipped past her to the door of the house.

Easing inside, he went through the big house to the dining room. Baldwin and Roweena Colensworth were seated at a long, polished oak table. George was standing off to one side, and a servant was placing food before each of them. Taking a deep breath, Orem put a hand on his gun, removed his hat, and entered the room.

Colensworth had a bite of food halfway to his mouth and stopped in mid-motion. He stared at Orem as if he were seeing a ghost. He seemed unable to speak.

Roweena suffered no such problem. When she spotted Orem, she came straight to her feet.

"What the blazes do you think you're doing here?" she snapped. "Baldwin! Call the men!"

Orem raised a hand to silence their protest. "I only came here for a word with you, Colensworth. I don't want any trouble."

The man bristled and rose to a standing position. "Trouble is going to be your first name, Clancy. You stole a slave from me. That will get you either dead or a prison sentence. Which will it be? I'll leave the choice up to you!"

"Togg showed up on the Texas side of the border. I hired him to work for me, but I aim to pay you a fair price for his contract."

"Bah! Who are you trying to fool with that story? You came and took that slave from the tanning shed. You busted Matt's jaw and nose doing it too."

"Like I said, I want to make things right. The last time they held an auction at Galveston, the average price of a top field hand was about fifteen hundred dollars. I'll pay you two thousand for Togg's contract."

"Don't you do it, Baldwin!" Roweena was red-faced with rage. "I want this high-handed, ignorant boor to pay for his crimes. There'll be no deals for Togg. You turn him over to us, Clancy, and we'll consider dropping the bounty on your head. Try and fight us and you'll end up in a graveyard!"

As he suspected, Roweena was the biggest obstacle in finding any peaceful resolution to his problems. With a patience he did not feel, Orem turned his attention to her.

"Be reasonable about this, ma'am. Togg

is safely in Texas. I can have a judge make a ruling and then I might end up with the man for less than the going price of a slave. Considering that you were going to kill the fellow, you don't have a leg to stand on. I'm trying to sort this out to benefit everyone."

Roweena bored into him with hot, smoldering eyes. Her teeth were anchored to make her face an ugly, vicious mask. Lost was the beauty of her years. She was more of an enraged animal, ready to snarl and lash out with her claws and teeth.

"Never, Clancy!" she hissed. "You're a dead man! If Jace was here, he'd cut your heart out and feed it to the dogs!"

Orem tried to reason with The Bull once more. "I'm trying to do what is right, Colensworth. Let me purchase Togg for a fair price. If he hadn't escaped, he'd be dead now and worth nothing to you. I'm offering you a chance to come out ahead on the deal."

The man's expression was granite. Hate oozed from his eyes, and his fists were clenched at his sides.

"Run for your life, Orem Clancy. You

won't get a second chance. Togg will soon be a dead man. The two of you can be buried in the same hole. That ought to be a lesson to any other white man who loves slaves. You John Browns are born to be hanged!"

Even as Orem sought words to pacify the man, Roweena left the table. She went over to the door and opened it.

"Matt! Clay!" she shouted at the top of her lungs. "Come running!"

Orem knew when a plan had been a total failure. He backed out of the room and ran toward the back door. A man appeared out of nowhere, his gun drawn, searching with his eyes.

Lowering his shoulder, Orem drove into him, knocking him off his feet. The man landed on his back, and unprepared for the fall, he couldn't get a decent hold on Orem. He clawed at Orem's legs but missed.

Orem bolted out the back door and raced around the barn. He grabbed his horse and took hold of the pommel to swing up onto his back. But something was wrong. Instead of his body being propelled up from the strength of his pull on the saddle horn, it came sliding off the horse's back. Orem wound up flat on his back, the saddle on top of him. Before he could recover, a gun was in his face.

"Rest easy, Clancy." A familiar voice was speaking from the opposite end of the rifle. "Twitch one muscle and the devil will be shaking your hand before morning."

There was some shouting and people running about. Before Orem could figure a way to escape, the man he'd knocked down arrived. It was Matt. He had recovered his gun and now pointed it at Orem.

"So you got him, Clay. Good work."

"What'll we do with him, Matt?"

"Let's take our man back into the house. I've a notion that Baldwin would like some words with him."

"Stone-cold dead, Clancy," Clay informed Orem. "That's what you're going to be before Baldwin is done."

Orem had no choice. He got slowly to his feet and let the two men remove his gun. Then he was prodded from behind, forced back toward the house.

"I cut the cinch on his saddle," Clay

said, chuckling. "You ought to have seen him trying to swing up onto his bronc."

Matt laughed at that. "Bet he about dug his spurs into the sky."

"Yeah, he looked as if he was trying to catch a ride on the wind. I seen a man slip out of the dark and speak to Sarah. When he sneaked into the house, I backtracked him until I found the horse. I'd say that this is the end of our slave-stealing banker from across the border."

Matt glared at Clancy. "Right you are, Clay. We warned him never to set foot on Diamond Head. Too bad Jace isn't here. He'd have enjoyed having a few words with him."

Walking with his hands up even with his shoulders, Orem had no chance. He looked quickly about, but there was no help, no escape. He was in trouble up to his neck this time. The twisted knot in his stomach told him that he was very close to death. Worse, he had nothing to bargain with. The two-thousand-dollar bank draft did not mean a thing to a man like Colensworth. What he would want was Orem's life. With Roweena egging him on, he would want Orem to die long and hard.

Chapter Ten

*J*amie faced the three men and awaited their decision.

Kip Jones was the unspoken leader of the trio. He took charge and began to ask questions.

"When did Orem leave?"

"The same time I did. He'll have reached the plantation by early this evening."

"And he was going to try and buy Togg from Baldwin Colensworth?"

"Yes."

"He went alone?"

"That's correct."

Kip groaned and looked at the other two. "Our boss just got himself into a pile of trouble. He doesn't have any idea of how tough that man can be. Colensworth will sure enough skin his hide and tan it in the sun."

"He went and got himself in real trouble," Togg said solemnly. "He went there to help me. He's going to end up dead on my account."

"We've got to do something right now!" Jamie urged the three men.

"No time," Kip replied. "Before we could get word to his father, he'd be food for the vultures."

"There must be something we can do." Jamie kept after them.

Kip looked over at Henry Brown. The man was loading a rifle. He was a man of few words, but he didn't wait to act.

"Now hold on, Henry! We can't go riding onto a plantation like white men. We try something like that, and we'll be hanged from the highest tree in the state."

Henry shook his head. "Are we free men or not, Kip? Orem did for us—we got to do for him."

Togg's look was one of incredulity. "You don't mean it? We'll ride up to Diamond Head and rescue Orem?"

"Henry ain't thinking straight." Kip was

shaking his head. "Black men don't attack white men. We can't go up against The Bull of Louisiana."

"I'll go with you!" Jamie cried. "We've got to be there if Orem gets into trouble."

"You don't even look like a woman," Kip said, growing flustered. "They might shoot you too, dressed the way you are, wearing that man's hat!"

"I owe Orem a great deal," she replied evenly. "Maybe I owe him as much as you men. I won't stand by and let him get killed."

Togg licked his lips, naked fear on his face. "Maybe Orem got away from the plantation all right. Could be that he got in and out without any trouble."

"Then we'll only have to ride until we meet up with him," Henry said. "I don't care what you two men do. My mind is made up. I'll be leaving with the lady here."

Kip threw up his hands in exasperation. "Henry, you think with your heart instead of your head!"

"I'm going," Henry repeated his intentions.

"You are more stubborn than those mustangs we been breaking!"

Henry had his rifle loaded. He headed toward the corral and the horses.

"Hold on there, Henry!" Kip shook his head and followed after him. "I'm thinking that I'll have to tag along and keep you out of trouble. You might get us both killed, but I'm going with you."

Togg stepped forward and swallowed hard. He had been a slave at Diamond Head. He had the most to fear from Colensworth and his men. To return to the plantation might mean a swift end to his dreams of a life as a free man. But not to go with Kip and Henry would be to remain a slave to himself. Orem had told him that he had to respect others and himself. He had responsibilities. That meant doing what was right, regardless of the consequences.

"I'll go along with you men," he said in a shaky voice. "It might mean our deaths, but I'm the reason Orem is in this mess."

Jamie waited for the three men to get horses for the four of them and a handful of supplies. She paced anxiously about and looked at the darkness of the sky. Orem would have reached the plantation by this time. He might have waited until dark to move in, but he'd undoubtedly made his appearance by now. If shooting started, he might already be wounded and dying.

No! Don't even think those thoughts! she scolded herself. Orem was careful. He knew the danger he was in. Probably all this fuss and worry was for nothing. Orem might be back in Blackwater before they even passed through town. Jim had promised to ride with them. He might arrive along the trail at any minute and tell her that everything was all right. They might be rushing about and getting ready all for nothing.

Trying to keep her thoughts positive didn't help. Jamie feared that Orem was in real trouble. His sense of honor was going to be the end of him.

Hadn't he seen how narrow-minded people could be over the slavery issue? He had helped to cut most of the hair right from her head, all because she dared to speak out against slavery. If they would dare to tar and feather a woman newspaper publisher, they would not hesitate to kill a man.

Orem had the dangerous misconception that all people had some good in them, that they could be reasoned with. Jamie had not been able to reason with the men and women that attacked her. They had burned everything she owned, then humiliated her in the worst possible way. Where was the goodness and common sense of those people?

Within a matter of minutes, the four of them were riding hard toward Blackwater. They would have Jim James waiting with fresh horses. Jim had known Kip and Henry would ride out to help Orem, regardless of the danger. He had dispatched Jamie to get them while he tried to round up some local help. Considering the opposition, that made the task more difficult. Baldwin Colensworth was a name to be reckoned with. No one wanted to take on The Bull of Louisiana.

"How long before we reach Blackwater?" Kip was alongside Jamie.

"I made the ride out to the ranch in about six hours. However, I didn't know exactly where to find it. We might make better time going back."

Kip showed a grave concern. "Then we've got a four- or five-hour ride out to Diamond Head. I don't like it. We won't make it to the plantation until well after daylight. Might even be midmorning."

"We'll be in time," Jamie said firmly. "I can't see it any other way. We'll make it."

"Hope you're right, ma'am. I sure hope you're right."

Jace came awake to someone shaking his shoulders. He stretched and looked up at Lars.

"What is it?"

"A lone rider came pounding horseflesh a little after dark. Couldn't tell much about him from the distance, but he was slight of build—maybe a kid."

"So then what?"

"He went in and met with the three blacks. Next thing I know, all four of them are riding off toward Blackwater as if someone had set fire to their horses' tails."

"This time of night?"

"Queer, ain't it?"

Jace rubbed the stubble on his jaw. "I wonder what's going on."

"You think Clancy might have heard about us crossing into Texas and sent for them?"

"Naw. He wouldn't send for some ex-slaves. What good would they be in a fight?"

"We seen them practicing this afternoon. Looks as if they've learned to shoot."

"No black man is going to kill a white man. It'd get a hundred of their own people slaughtered."

"Maybe not. That fellow Lincoln is talking about an end to slavery. What if they've made some kind of law to free the blacks and we ain't heard about it?"

"There would be a lot of talk first. We'd have heard about any such law before now." Jace pulled on his boots. "I think these three hands of Clancy's have to be acting on their own. I'm guessing he spotted something at Blackwater and wants some help. Might even be someone trying to collect the bounty Pa put on his head."

"What'll we do?"

"Let's saddle up. We'll head to Blackwater and see what's going on."

"This life on the trail ain't much fun,

Jace. I'm glad I never took to punching cattle. The ground don't get no softer with age."

"Soon as we finish our business with Clancy, we'll knock off for a few days and have us a high time in style. That suit you?"

"Yeah, Jace. That would suit me just fine."

"Get saddled up. The sooner we get rid of that banker, the sooner you can have a clean bed and a roof over your head."

Chapter Eleven

*S*tripped to the waist, Orem had his hands tied securely. The thick, round post was rough against his bare chest. He did not struggle, for there was no escape from his predicament. The early-morning sun was warm on his exposed back, but he knew the comfort would not last for very long.

"I've been wanting to see this since you pushed me into the river, Orem Clancy!" Roweena said, moving in front of him to look at his face. "I swore that I would get even with you for that disgrace. Now I'm going to watch you bawl like a baby!"

Orem turned his head slightly from side to side, subtly working to loosen the cords that were about his wrists.

"You know that falling into the river

was an accident, ma'am. If you'd been civil about my trying to help you, that dress would not have been ruined."

"How silly of me." She put on an innocent face. "Of course you were blameless. It was all my fault."

"I didn't say that."

"Well, Orem Clancy, you can cry out your innocence all you want. It won't make any difference. Clay handles a whip like most men handle a fork at the dinner table. He can cut the top off a carrot without touching the vegetable. I dare say he will take his time making you pay for your insolence."

"I came here to settle things with honor." Orem knew he was wasting his breath. "You and Baldwin should have listened to reason. This can only make matters worse."

She scoffed at that retort. "Worse for you. I'm going to sit back and sip a nice cup of tea. I'll enjoy every minute of entertainment you can offer us."

"I hope I don't disappoint you," he said, grunting cynically.

She laughed and walked away. He could

no longer see her movements but was aware of the sounds behind him. She was taking a seat in a chair some distance back. Then he heard footsteps approach and stop nearby.

"Matt would rather be doing this, Clancy, but a broken jaw limits a man's activities. I've never used a whip on a white man. Guess we'll see if black hide is any tougher than yours."

"Whatever you do now, remember that I'll not forget it. Justice has a way of coming to the surface. You hold the whip now, but the tables can turn."

Clay laughed at his words. "Keep on talking, Clancy. Talk until the pain turns your words to screams. I've had a few tough characters hitched to the whipping post. One of them died rather than cry out. If you want mercy from Mrs. Colensworth, you'd better cry out long and hard after a few lashes."

Orem set his teeth. "She can go to the devil!"

"Get to it, Clay!" Roweena shouted. "I want to hear him squeal like a stuck pig!"

The man chuckled in Orem's ear. "Like I said, Clancy, no mercy."

Orem didn't reply. He took several deep breaths and locked his hands together. His muscles tensed for the strike of the whip. He didn't know how much he could stand, for he had never been beaten in such a fashion. To cry out was to give Roweena her satisfaction. To keep silent was to suffer more punishment. He had no idea how much of a whipping Colensworth intended. They might only want to teach him a lesson with a few lashes, or it might be their intention to kill him. His fate was in their hands.

The whistle of the whip was like a deadly gust of wind. When the whip struck his back, it was like a clap of thunder. But the sting was that of a lightning bolt.

Orem sucked in his breath and arched his back against the sting of the whip. He gnashed his teeth and fought down the cry that rose to his lips.

Again there was the heinous whistle of the whip and the sickening *smack* of the cattail end cutting into flesh. The pain knifed through his back and shoulders, searing nerve endings like hot, burning irons. It was enough that his body twisted involuntarily.

Orem silenced himself with another burst of will. He suffered the pain and fought off the torment successfully. It cost him strength and he sagged against the ropes. Beads of sweat dotted his brow and began to trickle down along his ribs. His muscles were taut and rippled to ward off the bite of the lash.

How long could he hold out? How long before the cutting of the whip broke down his resistance and brought sobs to his lips? He didn't know. He only knew that to give in was to grant Roweena her sadistic satisfaction. It was fodder to his strength.

"Hit him harder!" the woman cried. "I want to hear him plead for his life!"

The wail of the whip cut the morning air again. Orem set himself to suffer the fire that ignited along his back. The force of the blow brought a groan to his lips, but he sealed it off with clenched teeth. His weight was against the ropes, his knees suddenly too weak to hold up his body. Tears filled his eyes until he could no longer see. Orem closed the lids tightly and concentrated on the next blow from the whip. He would need all of his power to quell off the cries that threatened to tear from his throat. He would die on the whipping post before he would give Roweena the satisfaction of hearing him cry out.

Jamie rode into the yard at a gallop. Jim James led the three other men from Clancy's ranch behind her. As a group, they pulled to a stop in a cloud of dust.

When Jamie saw Orem tied to the whipping post, she lost her composure.

"No!" she cried, half dismounting and half falling from her horse at the same time. "You filthy creatures! Stop!"

Even as she regained her feet and ran toward Orem, Jim and the others were facing off against Colensworth, Roweena, and their men.

"What's the meaning of this?" Colensworth was indignant. "How dare you men ride onto Diamond Head like a band of raiders!"

"We'll be taking Orem with us," Jim informed him. "If you try to stop us, there will be real trouble."

"He's threatening us, Baldwin!" Roweena was outraged. "Are you going to let him get away with that?"

But Matt and Clay knew they were outgunned. Jim had three black riders with him. All of them had guns and appeared ready to fight. With Lars and Jace away from the plantation, they had no chance against such odds.

"Why, that's Togg!" Roweena took a closer look at the men. "You get down off that horse this minute, Togg!"

Togg grew pale. The fear showed plainly on his face. Never had he dared to disobey the mistress of Diamond Head.

"No, ma'am," Kip said softly in Togg's defense. "He's not a slave. Orem Clancy brought you money to pay for him. He doesn't belong to you any longer. Once Togg pays Orem back a fair price, he'll be a free man."

Colensworth stepped up to confront the group. "You men are all in violation of the law. I'll have each and every one of you hanging from a tall tree. You, white trash," he said, pointing a finger at Jim. "I'll have you thrown in prison. Do you hear me?"

Henry pointed his gun at Colensworth. "Say that again, old man, and I'll blow a hole through you with this here rifle."

The Bull of Louisiana sputtered and looked at Jim. "You going to let a slave talk like that?"

"Kip and Henry are free men, Colensworth. They've got the same rights as you and me."

That put an incredulous look on his face. "You can't be serious. Those people are meant to serve, to be looked after like children. If you up and turn them loose, they'll come to ruin and take this country with them!"

Jamie worked to finally free Orem of the knots that held his hands. He collapsed, and Togg jumped down to lend a hand. She was not so concerned with Orem that she failed to see Togg exchange looks with a servant girl. Then he carried Orem over to a waiting horse. Flexing his powerful shoulders, he hefted Orem up into the saddle.

Jamie climbed up behind Orem. He was

only half conscious, but he sat under his own power.

"Why, you're a woman!" Roweena came closer to Jamie. "What on earth are you doing dressed like a man?"

"Excuse me, but I'm taking Orem back to Blackwater. If you have any questions, feel free to come speak to me there."

"You look like some . . . some beggar!" Roweena exclaimed. "What happened to your hair? And what's stuck to your skin?"

Jamie had to struggle to get hold of the reins. She held Orem in her arms, with his bloodied back leaning against her.

"This is the end for all of you!" Colensworth roared. "I'll have the law after you. We'll have a hundred men in the saddle by nightfall. You'd best clear out of the country, run as fast and far as you can!"

Togg looked again at Sarah. "We're leaving this place. I don't know when I can get back."

Sarah seemed to make up her mind. She crossed to Togg's side at a run. "Then I'm going with you."

"Sarah!" Roweena screamed. "Don't you dare leave with these filthy runaway slaves! I'll put you into the fields to work and suffer the heat. I'll watch your hide burn from the sun. I'll have you fed to the dogs!"

Togg lifted Sarah up into the saddle and swung up behind her. He looked at Colensworth, showing his first sign of courage.

"This woman is mine, Mr. Colensworth. I'll pay whatever you want for her, but she's going with me."

"All I want is your life, Togg," he said ominously. "I'll have it too."

Jamie pointed the horse for Blackwater.

"You won't get away with this," Clay warned Jim and the others. "I'll be seeing you boys again."

"Don't let anything but common sense and fear of death stop you," Jim replied. Then the group galloped out of the yard.

"How's he look?" Kip asked Jamie. "Appears he took about twenty lashes before we got there."

"He'll be all right," she said without reservation. "Once I get some salve and bandages on his back, he'll be fine."

"What about Colensworth's threats to

get even?" Kip asked. "He's mean and powerful. He'll do as he claims."

"Let's hope he waits until Orem is on the mend. If he comes after us with a hundred guns, we won't have a prayer," Jamie said.

"Too late to worry about that now," Kip said. "We'll have to see what steps Orem wants us to take. This is bound to start a real battle."

Jim glanced at their back trail and urged the group to more speed. "Orem is a respected man. Maybe the people in town will back him."

Jamie was not so optimistic. "When it comes to the slavery issue, Jim, we don't have an ally in Blackwater. Orem's earned more than a few enemies for making his stand."

"Regardless of what stand Orem has taken, he's the owner of our bank," Jim reminded her. "He lent every one of us enough to get started in business and he has been a friend. That deserves some consideration."

Jamie shook her head. "When it comes to a war, friends don't always stand at your side. We can't deny that we're helping slaves to escape, not with Sarah riding with us."

"Time has come for revolt," Henry said firmly. "Maybe we'll be the ones who start the war between the Southern states and those that support President Lincoln."

"That would be one short war," Kip said, snorting. "Three black men, a crazy newspaperwoman, a banker, and his best friend against the entire states of Texas and Louisiana."

Turning to other matters, Jim glanced at Togg. "How'd it feel, Togg, to face up to Colensworth?"

"Scared me to death," he answered honestly. "I don't think I'm ready to strike out on my own just yet. I came real close to climbing down and doing what Mrs. Colensworth told me. I never refused an order before."

"I—I didn't know what to do, either," Sarah said, her face showing her fear plainly. "I don't know how I ever got the courage to up and leave."

"You belong with me," Togg told her. "You and me will get married."

"If we live that long." Kip showed a genuine concern. "No slave has ever walked off The Bull's place and lived to tell about it. We just crossed one of the most power-ful men in the country."

Henry grinned. "Too late to worry now. Orem will have a plan. You wait and see."

Jim exchanged looks with Jamie. "Think your man can figure a way out of this mess for all of us?"

Jamie felt a glowing inside. Jim had called Orem *her* man. "I want to get him patched up first. Then we'll pile all this on his shoulders and see if he buckles at the knees."

"It sure don't look good to me, Jamie," Jim replied. "I'll ask around town once we reach Blackwater, but the slavery issue is a hot poker. Touch it and you get burned. I'm afraid we've got hold of it with both hands."

Jamie held Orem tightly. He was sitting upright, but he was more unconscious than awake. His head was tipped until his chin rested against his chest. He was riding out of memory, not because he knew what he was doing.

"There must be a way," she said, more to herself than to Jim. "There has to be a way."

Chapter Twelve

*R*oweena cursed and stormed about the house. She would not be consoled. Her pride had been shattered by the appearance of the slaves and the people from town. She wanted revenge and she wanted it right away.

"I'm going to speak to the governor," Colensworth said in an attempt to soothe her. "There are a number of legal steps we can take against Clancy and the others."

"For heaven's sake, Baldwin! I don't want the governor to send us a letter of sympathy and maybe reprimand Clancy for being a bad boy. I want to see his blood soaking up the dirt! I want him to suffer!"

"We gave him a pretty good beating." Clay spoke up for the first time. "You saw that he had passed out from the whipping, Mrs. Colensworth."

She glared at the hired man with hot, burning eyes. "He didn't even cry out—not once!"

"The guy is tough, but it hurt him all the same."

"It isn't enough! Look at how they came riding in and took command of our plantation. They dared to come here armed and ready to fight. They took my servant girl right out from under our noses. We can't let them get away with something like that. The next thing you know we'll be in a war with an army of slaves!"

"You're right about that," Colensworth agreed. "We need to show the country that we won't tolerate such acts. I don't intend to have something like that happen ever again."

Roweena's expression showed an instant satisfaction. "Good for you, Baldwin. What do you have in mind?"

"Soon as Jace and Lars return, I think they ought to join Matt and Clay. The four of them should ride into Blackwater, make an example of that James fellow and see

what our banker is up to. We have to return a show of strength, or we may become
the laughingstock of the state."

"I want the hide of that girl too!"

"There was a story about some woman
newspaper publisher being tarred and
feathered in Shreveport," Clay interjected.
"It looked like our female visitor had suffered a fate like that."

"That's right!" Roweena understood immediately. "She was spouting off against
slavery and stirring up trouble. I remember
now." She slammed her fist into the palm
of her hand. "That's why she had her hair
cut off and had black splotches on her skin.
She's the one, all right."

"Then Orem has aligned himself with
Lincoln and the North. He's a traitor to
our country," Colensworth said.

"How about we do this up right?" Matt
was grinning at the thought. "We'll have
a party for those slave lovers. We'll tar and
feather them all."

"Only do it right this time," Roweena
suggested. "Hot, boiling tar and enough
feathers that they'll never come clean.
Then ride Orem out on a rail!"

"That could be risky. Orem has friends in Blackwater."

"Find some of those antislavery newspapers that woman put out. Stick them up on the walls, get the people behind you. Round up some men from the other plantations. You can get together an army."

"We'll get started on it right away." Matt grinned, still showing a crooked smile. His jaw had not healed completely. "This ought to be fun."

Even as the two men ran to get their horses, Colensworth came to stand beside his wife.

"I wonder if our intentions will be understood, Roweena. We need to keep the support of the people in this state."

"You've never worried about what anyone else thought about your actions, Baldwin. Why the concern all of a sudden?"

"I've kept abreast of the news. There are a good many people who admire that man Lincoln. Even the states that are threatening to secede from the Union have mixed support. I wonder if those people who don't have slaves will be ready to go to war to keep our way of life intact."

"You talk about the strangest things, Baldwin. Anyone with any sense knows that these slaves could never feed and clothe themselves. They need to be taken care of."

But Colensworth's face showed a new look of concern. "You saw how Togg spoke to me. He sounded almost like a free white man. And what about your servant, Sarah? She had the courage to walk out right in front of you."

"Nonsense." She laughed at his misgivings. "Orem has convinced a couple of slaves that they are free men—that's all there is to it. If we put an end to Orem, we put an end to those stupid ideas."

"I want that black man beaten," Colensworth said tightly. "He spoke to me as if he was every bit as good as me. I want him beaten to death."

Roweena put a hand on his arm, her face warming with a smile. "Jace will see to it. Jace and the others will put an end to Orem and any thoughts of freedom for blacks. You'll see. Everything will be back to normal just as soon as that banker and the others are punished good and proper."

*   *   *

Orem spent two days healing from the beating. Jamie was the perfect nurse, applying ointment to his back and tending to his every whim. On the third morning, Orem managed to get a shirt on and tuck it into his waistband. The welts on his back had scarred over, but his muscles were still stiff and sore from the beating. Still, after he shaved and combed the hair out of his face, he looked back to his old self.

Kip and Henry returned to Orem's ranch, while Togg and Sarah remained in town to help out. Jim put them up in back rooms of the hotel and gave them some chores to keep busy. Togg intended to be there only until Orem was up and about. He and Sarah wanted to be properly married before anything happened.

The ruckus started early that third morning. Copies of the news article Jamie had written in Shreveport were tacked up all over town. Word of mouth had been enough to give her a reputation, but no one had seen her work in print. It didn't take long for the news story to draw considerable criticism from the people in town.

By the time Orem reached the street, there were groups of people gathered about. They were discussing Jamie's point of view with little favor. Here was a woman from the North, trying to blame the Southern states for enslaving an innocent race of people. She dared to compare Southerners to Romans and slander their respectability. Togg spotted Orem and hurried to meet him. The man's brow was drawn in worry.

"There's trouble coming, Orem," he said, keeping his voice low enough that no bystanders could hear.

Orem was aware that a number of people were pointing and looking his way. Togg was a runaway slave, Jamie was a slave sympathizer, and Orem was protecting them both. The people were openly questioning his loyalties.

"You ought to head for the ranch, Togg. Things might get ugly."

Togg risked a glance at the angry faces. "I've never been a free man, Orem. But Kip and Henry keep telling me I got to learn. If this trouble is because of me, I should stick by you."

Orem had to smile. He knew Togg had

been a slave in most ways, but not in his heart. Inside, he was free. He did not yet know how to act like a free man, but he was ready to accept his share of the suffering to learn.

"Where is Jamie?" Orem asked.

"She and Jim are in the café. They didn't think you would be up and around for at least another day."

"Did you see who put up the newspapers?"

"Matt and Clay. I saw Lars and Jace ride into town early too. They been talking to people and getting support. I think we're facing a mob."

"Go tell Jim and Jamie that I want to see them. We'll meet at the rear of Jim's place. I've got to stop by the bank and see what has been going on."

Orem felt a chill from the people on the street. There were some who sent oaths and dirty names floating after him. The town was ready to explode.

At the bank, he saw the line of people at the tellers' windows. Johnson was there to meet him. He showed no hostility, but held a ledger in his hand.

"Thirty-eight accounts have been closed already, Mr. Clancy. We're running short of funds."

"Remember that the people who owe us money can't close their accounts until we have been repaid. That will slow some of them down."

"What are you going to do?"

Orem let out a sigh. "I'm putting you in charge till further notice. Keep the windows open unless you run out of money. Call in the loans to keep up your cash flow. We don't want the bank to fail."

"You didn't answer my question. What about you?"

"I've got to visit the governor and see if I can work this out. Until something is done, I won't be coming into Louisiana."

"From the rumors, I think you had best leave the state as fast as you can."

"Good luck, Johnson. I know you can handle things here."

"Thank you. I'll do my best."

Orem left the bank, jeers following after him from the people he passed. The time had come to get out of the state. Colensworth would have the law on his side.

Sarah had run away from the plantation, and Orem's men had pointed guns at The Bull himself. There wasn't a plantation owner in the country who wouldn't back Colensworth. He could raise an army against Orem.

Orem was stiff from his beating, but his strength was coming back. If he could slip quietly out of town, he might be able to avoid any real trouble. Name-calling hurt his pride, but it wasn't going to break his bones.

"Where you going, Clancy?" A man's coarse, booming voice stopped him like a stone wall.

Turning slowly about, Orem found Lars Sweeny and Jace Colensworth squared off against him. He felt his heart sink into his stomach.

"We've some unfinished business, Clancy," Jace said, flashing a wicked grin. "Lars here wants to see how many of your bones he can break."

At his best, Orem did not consider himself a match for the mountain of a man. In his present condition, he wouldn't last two minutes.

Jace had his hand on his gun. He appeared ready to draw. He could get off a shot before Orem managed to remove the thong from his own gun. He had no chance to draw.

The big Swede raised his meaty paws and came forward. "I'm going to mash your face like a bowl of taters, Clancy. When I get done, no one is even going to recognize you."

Orem had no options. He shook loose his muscles and brought his fists up to a fighting position. . . .

Chapter Thirteen

*T*ogg was going back to the hotel. He saw the crowd and glimpsed Orem in the middle. He knew Orem was in trouble. Jim and Jamie had gone out the back way, so they were too far away to help. Seeing Jace on the walk, he knew there was no one to stop the trouble.

Moving closer, Togg could see the action. Orem was ducking and jabbing at Lars Sweeny. He was about half the size of Lars. The big man shook off his weak blows and clubbed him with huge fists. Orem went down, but Lars dragged him to his feet and worked him over some more. He was going to kill him.

Togg stood for a long moment. His training was hard to forget. *Never look a white man in the eye, keep your mouth shut, do what you're told,* he remembered. It was ingrained in him from childhood. He didn't know how to be a free man.

But he started forward slowly. Togg was thirty pounds lighter than Lars, but he was strong as an ox. He had worked long and hard all his life. He had endurance and a relentless tenacity that kept him from quitting. He owed Orem his very life. He could not stand back and let him be beaten to death.

Orem took a blow to the head and bounced off the wall of a nearby building. He sank to his knees, bleeding about the nose and mouth, gasping for breath. He couldn't last much longer.

Togg pushed through the crowd and stepped between Orem and Lars. In a voice that was as strong as he could manage, he dared to meet the bully eye to eye.

"He's had enough, Lars. You proved that you can beat a man who hasn't recovered from being whipped."

"Will you get him!" Jace said, laughing scornfully. "Togg sounds like a free man. Ain't that something?"

"I'll be taking Orem to his room," Togg informed the crowd.

But Lars took a menacing pose in front of him. "Only if you can get past me, slave."

Togg swallowed hard, but he refused to back down. "I got to take Orem to his room, Lars. Don't make me fight you."

Lars laughed. "A slave? You're going to fight me?"

Togg knotted his fists. He had fought before, but most of it had been in fun. There was no fun in facing off against Lars, none whatsoever.

Before Togg could set himself, Lars charged into him. Togg grunted from a punch to his kidneys. Then a brutal fist smacked him above the eye. Lars pounded at him, trying to beat him into the street. The crowd was yelling and shouting their approval.

Togg took the man's punishment and drew strength from the pain. He mustered an inner courage and sent a fist at Lars. When it connected, the crowd grew instantly silent.

Lars backed off, shaking his head. There

was blood coming from his nose. Togg had hurt him with that blow.

They circled and came together like two bulls butting heads. Both of them flailed with doubled fists, slamming punches into the other. Togg was solid and lean. He hardly felt the jabs. He got his second wind and turned the tide.

Lars backed up, covering his face with his fists. Togg drove at him, pounding at his exposed stomach. When Lars dropped his guard, Togg's knuckles exploded right between the man's eyes. It sent him reeling backward.

Togg kept after him, slugging away. He took out all his hostility against the slavers. He hammered Lars until the man went down. Then he stood over him, daring him to get up.

Lars was done. He groaned and rolled onto his stomach. He lacked the strength to rise again.

Togg lowered his fists and looked around. The people were looking at him with a mixture of fascination and puzzlement. He didn't know what they were thinking. At that moment, he didn't care. Orem was still on the ground.

"I'm taking Orem to his hotel room," Togg said, winded from the fight. "I don't want anyone to try to stop me."

Jace had his hand on his gun, but he seemed undecided as to what to do. While he made up his mind, Togg lifted Orem up into his arms and carried him toward the hotel.

Jamie and Jim had since reached the building. They both hurried out to see what had happened.

"It's all right," Togg told them. "I got Orem. He'll be okay."

Orem came awake with a start. He sat up so quickly that the world spun and went black before his eyes. He put a hand to his head and waited for it to clear.

"Anyone see the driver of that stage? I think he ran over my face with both the team and wagon!"

"Lars was driving the stage." Jamie's voice was close by.

Orem shook the clouds from his mind

and located the young woman. She was sitting next to his bed.

"We've got to get out of here," Orem said immediately, still shaking the cobwebs from his head. "Jace and his boys will come with guns the next time."

"At least you won't have to worry about your bank anymore." Jamie had a sour note in her voice.

"Why is that?"

"It was burned to the ground a couple of hours back. Jim figures this place is next. Most of the windows have already been broken."

Orem could see Jamie clearly. She was doing her best to mask her fear, but she was scared. Her complexion was pale, she wrung her hands nervously, and her eyes were wide and full of terror.

"Where are Togg and Sarah?"

"Downstairs with Jim. They're in the back, staying away from open windows. Togg is sure to be a target, after what he did to Lars."

That made Orem take notice. "What he did to Lars?" he repeated.

"He beat him in a fair fight," Jamie said proudly. "He saved your life."

"And he whipped Lars?"

She smiled at his incredulous look. "Togg Jackson is no longer a slave in his heart, Orem. He's a free man."

"Well, he'll be a dead man if we don't get out of here and do it darn quick."

"I think you're right about that. The crowd has grown more ugly all day long."

"Did you see who was behind setting fire to my bank?"

"Jace had a hand in it. I think most of the work was done by the men from Diamond Head, but no one tried to stop them. That in itself says a great deal."

Orem let out a pronounced sigh. "Yes, it does. If they will let the bank be burned to the ground, they'll stand back and watch any or all of us be killed. We've got to get out of here."

"What do you want us to do?"

"Have Jim gather up five horses. I think he has worn out his welcome in Blackwater too. We'll ride down to my father's bank in Kanterville. We can decide what we're going to do then."

"By 'we,' I suppose you mean all of us."

He smiled at her. "Especially you and me."

It was Jamie's turn to smile. "You've kissed me only once. I thought you might have felt sorry for me at the time."

"I told you that I wasn't thinking of you, but of myself."

"Really?"

"Lean a little closer and I'll show you."

Jamie sat on the edge of the bed. It was close enough that Orem was able to pull her into his arms. He kissed her soundly.

She leaned back and smiled. "You did that as if you meant it, Orem. Are there any words that go with such an overture?"

"How about I love you?"

Her eyes shone brightly. "That will do for a start. Shall we get out here?"

"Unless we want to get roasted in the next bonfire, that would seem the best solution."

"I'll tell the others."

He watched her hurry from the room. Then he stiffly got his boots and hat. He strapped on his Spiller and Burr pistol and checked the load. He had no illusions about leaving Blackwater. Jace and the other men from Diamond Head were in town. There might be trouble. If it came, it would not be a fistfight. Jace had killed before. He would be the one to worry about.

Orem did not concern himself about his belongings. The incident at Colensworth's plantation had escalated to a war. He had to get his people out before the killing started.

Chapter Fourteen

*R*oweena climbed out of the carriage before Baldwin could even get down to help. George held the horses steady and awaited instructions.

"Hitch up the rig," Roweena told him. "I'm going to find my son and see what has been going on."

"Wait for me, Roweena," Colensworth said. "There's nothing happening right now. The town is as peaceful as a grave-yard."

But she hurried off toward the lights of the nearest saloon. She had never entered such an establishment, but she knew she could stand at the door and see if her son or one of their men was in the place.

Colensworth hurried to keep up with her. He was laboring to catch his breath when she stopped just inside the saloon doors. She waved to Jace and caught his attention.

Jace looked up from a table and gave her a questioning look. "What's the matter?" he asked as he walked over to her.

"Nothing is the matter," she replied. "I want to know what you've done so far."

He pointed up the street. "See the bank? It's cinders. We burned it to the ground."

"Excellent!" Roweena cried. "How about the banker? Was Orem Clancy in the bank at the time?"

Jace's expression clouded. "He was laid up from the beating that Lars gave him."

"Good! Good!"

But her son didn't appear happy. "And Lars is laid up from the beating Togg gave him."

Roweena's eyes grew round and full of shock. "What? Togg? *Our* Togg?"

"Didn't know the slave was capable of it. He took everything Lars threw at him and came back strong. He almost beat Lars to death."

Colensworth glowered. "See what I've been saying? Our slaves are turning on us—all because of these stupid ideas Lincoln has put into people's heads!"

"Clay is watching the hotel," Jace informed them. "That's where Clancy and the others have taken refuge."

"I want him, Jace," Roweena screamed. "I want that man dead!"

"We'll get to him, just as soon as—"

They turned as a group. Clay was running up the street toward them. He slid to a stop and directed his words at Jace.

"They're making a run for it! I saw Jim James bringing up a bunch of horses. They're going to try and get out under the cover of darkness."

Roweena grabbed her husband's gun. "No, they won't! I won't let them leave!"

"Hold on there, woman!" Colensworth tried to retrieve his gun from her. She jerked away and started toward the hotel. He had to run to keep up.

"Where's Matt?" Jace asked Clay.

"He's there. We've got them covered front and back."

"Wait!" Colensworth cried. "This is going to get some of us killed. Let's get some help!"

But Roweena had her mind made up. Orem had insulted her. Togg had dared to beat up Lars. Sarah had defied her in front of everyone on the plantation. There had to be an end to it. Orem, that busybody newswoman, Togg, and Sarah—they all had to pay!

Orem was on the stairs when Roweena crashed through the front door. Jace and Clay had their guns drawn. Before he could speak, they opened fire.

Orem dived for cover, clawing for his gun. He heard Jim's shout from downstairs and then more shots.

Raising up, Orem returned fire at Jace and Clay. He missed the first shot, but his second hit Clay square. It backed him right out the door. When he stepped off the porch, he fell onto his back.

A bullet chipped wood near Orem's face. He used the banister for what cover it offered and sent another bullet at Jace.

Jim fired from below as Roweena stormed right through the building. She was oblivious to the shooting, waving her gun about, screaming that she was going to kill Togg, Sarah, Jamie, and Orem.

She was lost to his sight, but Jace was hit in the leg. Baldwin remained out on the porch. He had picked up Clay's gun, but he didn't enter the hail of bullets.

There was a volley of shots from below. Then Matt came through the back of the house. He looked first at Jace, then spun about to search for Orem. It gave Orem time to take aim.

A slug tore through Matt's chest. He staggered back into the counter and slumped to the floor.

"Your time!" Jace shouted at Orem. "It's your time, Clancy!"

The young Colensworth came limping to the foot of the stairs. He fired at Orem, pulling the trigger again and again.

Orem felt a white-hot path scorch along his ribs. A second bullet whistled past his ear. He returned fire, knowing he was spending his last round.

Jace took a bullet low in the chest. He folded forward and went to his knees. Then he went over backward and rolled to the bottom of the stairs.

Orem rose up slowly, his smoking gun still in his hand. He felt a dampness against his shirt from where he'd been grazed by Jace's bullet. He started down the stairs, wondering how many others had been killed or wounded.

Roweena came charging back into the room. She looked at Matt, then out the door at Clay. Last, she fixed her attention on Jace.

"No!" she screamed. "No!"

Orem began to back slowly up the steps. He could see blood in the woman's eyes. She turned her gun toward him.

"You rotten, vile snake! You killed my son!"

Orem searched for an exit. He was too far from the top of the stairs. He put a hand on the railing. If he could jump to the lower floor, she might miss her first shot.

"I'm going to kill you, Clancy!" Roweena was hysterical. "Die, you dirty, stinking coyote! Die!"

The sound of a gun filled the room with a blast. Orem flinched, knowing the woman could not miss from fifteen feet. He was prepared for the bullet's impact. . . .

Roweena's eyes were the size of silver dollars. She opened her mouth and tried to form a word. Then the hand holding the gun dropped to her side. She stared at a small hole in the bodice of her gown.

Orem saw Jamie then. She had a gun in her hand. He realized that she had shot Roweena.

Colensworth came in at a run. He caught Roweena as she collapsed. The man fell under her weight but cradled her head in his lap.

"Blast you and your slaves, Clancy!" he cried. "You've killed my wife and son!"

Orem went down the steps. He holstered his gun and discovered that Jamie was at his side. Her face was ashen.

"I—I didn't know what else to do. She shot Jim. She shot at me." She raised up a bloody left arm. "She was going to kill us all."

Orem guided Jamie out of the room. Togg had been knocked unconscious by Matt, but Sarah had brought him around. Jim was not so lucky. Roweena had killed him.

The sounds of windows breaking and people shouting sent Orem and the others out into the darkness. They quickly mounted their horses and made their way out of town. By the time they were safely away, there was a blaze lighting the night sky.

"That will be the hotel," Orem said. "The people of Blackwater have decided which side of the slavery issue they are going to back."

"They're wrong," Jamie murmured. "Slavery is wrong. There are no two ways about it."

"It's a long way to the ranch. I think we had better patch up the bleeding as best we can and get moving. Very likely there will be a lot of bloodthirsty men on our trail before long."

"What will we do?" Togg asked.

"Whatever we have to do," Orem replied. "That's what a free man does, Togg."

"I'm beginning to learn that, Orem. I'm learning it right quick."

Chapter Fifteen

*D*earborne Clancy was solemn, looking very old for his years. He sat behind his desk and held up a piece of paper to read. It was the second time he had read it.

"Judge Devires has sent word, Orem. There is nothing he can do. The governor revoked his powers. Colensworth has the entire state up in arms. There is a very good chance that he will soon have Texas try to extradite you and the others."

Orem felt Jamie move closer. Her hand slipped down to take his own. Togg and Sarah were out in the lobby. Kip and Henry, whom they had met at Orem's ranch, had the horses around in back of the bank.

"Then I guess this is it, Father. I'm leaving the state and the banking business."

Dearborne nodded his agreement. "Your mother and I will miss you, son. Send us a wire once you are settled."

"Sorry about the bank at Blackwater."

His father shrugged. "It was mostly yours anyway. How's it feel to be broke?"

"I've still got the ranch. Any ideas on a buyer?"

Dearborne reached into his coat pocket and removed an envelope. He handed it to Orem.

"This is a bank voucher for the approximate worth of your ranch. I figured you would need something to start over with." He smiled at Jamie. "Especially now that you've decided to settle down and start a family."

"Thanks, Father. I appreciate that."

Dearborne raised his hand to stop any thanks. "I don't expect gratitude, son. You have the courage to do what you think is right. I admire that. From that night we were on that slave ship together, I have always wished that I had that kind of strength."

"It could be that seeing those people

drown is what made me so aware of their plight, Father. I don't really know."

"Head for Colorado. Denver is growing into a big town. They will be needing banks. If a war comes, Colorado is one of the territories the President will want to back his side. You'll do all right there. I'm told there are some blacks, but no slaves."

"Sounds like good advice."

"Don't come back here, son. Colensworth has put a price on your head. Once word reaches Texas, you won't be safe."

"I'll keep you and Mother in my heart, Father."

Then Orem and Jamie, with Togg and Sarah, left the town of Kanterville behind them. Kip and Henry rode along. They were trained to work in several fields. If a war came, they were ready to fight for their people's freedom.

"We must look like an odd mixture," Jamie said. "A white couple, a black couple, and two free black men."

Orem took a last look over his shoulder. "We might come back someday, when all men are free."

"That has a wonderful sound, Orem. When all men are free!"